STAR WARS®

TALES FROM A GALAXY FAR, FAR AWAY

ALIENS

VOLUME I

WRITTEN BY
LANDRY Q. WALKER

ILLUSTRATED BY
TYLER SCARLET

DISNEP
LUCASFILM
PRESS

LOS ANGELES • NEW YORK

Printed in the United States of America

First Edition, April 2016

1 3 5 7 9 10 8 6 4 2

FAC-008598-16059

ISBN 978-1-4847-4141-2

Library of Congress Control Number on file

Reinforced binding

Designed by Gegham Vardanyan

Visit the official *Star Wars* website at: www.starwars.com.

HIGH NOON
ON JAKKU

CONSTABLE ZUVIO'S fingertips brushed the handle of the small blaster he kept hidden in a holster in the folds of his robe. "I don't want to do this, Seezee," the gray-skinned Kyuzo said, his voice clear through the bandages he wore over his mouth. "No one else has to be hurt. Not me . . . and not you."

The sun was low in the sky. The dry desert landscape of Jakku stretched around the pair for kilometers. To an outside observer, Zuvio and the droid designated CZ-1G5 might as well have been the only two entities on the planet.

CZ stood across the dune from the constable, his outline framed by the setting sun. With a slow and deliberate motion, the bone-white secretary droid began to raise the blaster pistol he held in his unlikely hand.

"Drop the blaster . . ." Zuvio warned, gripping his own small blaster tightly. He was fast . . . but CZ-1G5 was renowned for his speed. Could the constable raise his weapon in time?

"I'm sorry, sir," replied the droid in his perfect clipped speech, "but I have no other option."

A long silence hung in the air. The dry atmosphere of Jakku pressed heavily on the constable and the droid.

A single shot was fired.

And with that, only one figure was left standing, his shadow long with regret as the last remnants of day drifted away.

EARLIER.

Niima Outpost sat near the equator of Jakku, not far from the mountain ridge known as the Fallen Teeth. For Jakku, it was a relatively comfortable and temperate zone, with conditions that were mostly survivable. It was only in the peak hours of a few days of the year that you had to stay out of the sun altogether. On those days, the burning, punishing radiation of Jakku's star would fry the skin of even the most heat-resistant species.

It was one of those days.

Constable Zuvio sat at his desk, bored. The short and stocky Kyuzo looked almost comical at the tiny workstation, his wide-brimmed war helmet hiding his features in shade, his eyes darting back and forth as he examined a stack of documents. Zuvio was a stern-looking individual, with most of his features perpetually covered by bandages that helped his sensitive respiration system cope with the climate. His eyes were yellow with black slit-shaped pupils, and his brow was furrowed in an expression that made people think he was always angry. The secret truth of the matter was that Zuvio suffered from vision problems, common in Kyuzos, and his expression was formed from years of squinting slightly to see better.

On the harsh world of Jakku, better to let people believe he was angry.

The role of constable was a difficult one. Despite the fact that the population of the town was relatively small, there was always someone willing to take advantage of the slightest weakness in his or her neighbor. So, as is the case with any gathering of beings, a desire for a semblance of structure slowly arose among the prospectors and scavengers who had drifted to the crumbling settlement of rickety landing bays and dusty salvage yards. And somehow, amid that attempt at self-governance, Zuvio found himself pinned with the label of constable. It was a job that managed to keep the Kyuzo quite busy—mostly with incoming starships and the trouble they always seemed to bring.

That day was a rare one. The best kind: a quiet day. So instead of theft and assault to investigate or ship captains to interrogate, there was paperwork— long-overdue documents that needed to be read, signed.

Luckily, the outpost had an answer for that, too; the position of constable meant that Zuvio was permitted part-time use of Niima's lone secretary droid, CZ-1G5. CZ worked in an administrative capacity for several of the outpost's more prominent denizens. The droid was ancient by tech standards—probably over three hundred years old—and while there were more modern droids that might have been more competent, the small Western Reaches colony had never needed one better.

CZ entered the small office and moved through the room with practiced ease, quickly scanning the pile of paperwork the constable had submitted and filing it with the proper agency via his built-in long-wave comlink transmitter. It was a sight to behold, the droid moving at lightning pace, flipping through documents at a speed impossible for most biological entities to match. Zuvio watched the droid out of the corner of his eye, listening to the sounds made by his quick movement. It was almost hypnotic.

It was a good thing the droid was around, too, as Zuvio's archaic preference for paper was impossible for any other droid to wrap its programming around.

"You're late, Seezee," Zuvio said brusquely.

The droid did not immediately answer, instead shuffling off to the hallway to enter his security clearance codes into Zuvio's encryption terminal. Data-locked terminals like that were a common way to keep secure forms protected, and typically only the owners could access them. CZ had a modified transmitter that allowed interface. It was a necessary step on Jakku, as few other beings could be trusted with the codes but a second point of access was always needed in case of emergency.

"Not saying it's a problem, just not very like you," Zuvio continued. "Most of the time, you're where you're supposed to be, like clockwork." It was true. The two beings had worked closely together for years, and though Zuvio wasn't exactly the type to make friends, CZ was about as close to earning that label as any might ever get. A change in the droid's routine wouldn't be noticeable to many, but to Zuvio? It stood out like water in the desert.

The droid turned toward the constable. After his many decades in service, his mild, amiable voice was tinged with a mechanical hum.

"I'm so sorry, sir."

The constable was about to respond when the office shook from a loud explosion nearby.

B Y THE TIME Zuvio arrived on the scene, his two deputies were already scanning the area. A banking ship had been hit, and hit hard by the look of it. The banking ship was a regular transport that arrived at the outpost every cycle to manage transactions on behalf of the Western Reaches Exchange. It usually stayed three or four rotations, then left to conduct other business. The ship served as one of the few anchors between Niima Outpost and the rest of the galaxy, and a strike against it could have heavy repercussions. Though the ship was built to carry a modestly sized cargo, many of the transactions were done electronically, with a large computer core in the systems mainframe built to hold account information secure until the ship reached a point where the data could be transmitted to the larger Exchange network.

Whoever had struck the ship hadn't wanted to take any chances of failing. One side of the small cargo vessel was obliterated. That was the explosion Zuvio had heard—and the blast had taken out at least seven citizens and two droids.

A crowd was gathering. "Drego, Streehn," Zuvio addressed his two cousins. "Crowd control." The Kyuzo deputies moved to hold back the growing mass of concerned citizens.

One of them, an older green-skinned Rodian, wailed, "Our credits! Everything we had was on that transport!"

Another, a Melitto, shouted, "We'll be ruined! What will we do?" But both of them were abruptly pushed aside by a long-nosed and rather thin member of the Kubaz species, one wearing uncommonly long and very finely tailored robes. Uncommon for Jakku, anyway. It was clear at a glance that the Kubaz was no native of the barren world.

"Constable!" he said angrily through a handheld translator. "I demand to know what is happening here!"

The Kubaz in question was Rikard Lovas, and the banking transport that had been attacked belonged to him.

Zuvio waved the banker past the deputies. "It's a robbery," he declared in his flat voice. "The cargo hold is empty. And the computer core holds no records of any active accounts."

Lovas turned a pale blue-gray that looked sickly for his species. A bead of sweat escaped the thick rectangular goggles he always wore. "But . . ." he stammered. "But that's impossible! Our system is heavily encrypted. No one could possibly access it. Not without . . ."

Lovas glanced at a panel on the interior of the ship. It was just like the one in Zuvio's office. The one that allowed an individual with the correct codes to access encrypted data.

But outside of the bank manager, no one could have that access. No one except . . .

"Seezee . . ." whispered Zuvio. "Oh, no."

CZ-1G5 was gone by the time Zuvio returned to the Office of the Constable. Worse, the small locked armory in the office had been cleaned out. Three blasters. A sniper rifle. All the grenades. Even the vibro-pike he usually carried. Gone.

And a speeder was missing, as well.

The only weapon Zuvio had left was the small blaster he kept hidden at his desk. He checked it. The power cell was at half, and he had no time for a charge—not with a transport-robbing, heavily armed droid making off across the desert wastes.

And CZ would be out there, in the parched wasteland that covered the majority of the planet. The droid couldn't afford to stay on Jakku, and there wasn't a ship—not in Niima—that would take him. Zuvio didn't even need to check a map. The only logical direction for the rogue droid to head was south, toward the Fallen Teeth. There was an abandoned attempt at a settlement out there that pirates sometimes used to hide smuggling ships when they didn't want to pay docking fees.

That assumed the droid would act logically, of course. But none of it, Zuvio thought, none of it made any sense. CZ had served the town since the first colonists landed. Zuvio knew the droid well; he was liked and respected across the entire community. The droid was even known to volunteer in the public kitchens and work in his free time as a volunteer care provider for the ill. If there was something CZ wanted, all the droid had to do was ask. Why throw it all away now?

Time to find the droid and ask him.

Zuvio called in to Drego and Streehn, giving them orders to forward all evidence from the robbery to his personal comm system, and then jumped on one of the remaining speeders and headed south toward the Teeth.

I N THE WASTES OF JAKKU, south of the out-post, the droids waited. Zuvio was coming, and they had to be ready.

G2-9T distributed the weapons, a grinding noise emanating from its broken voice modulator as it did so. A BD-3000 with a deeply scarred and corroded chassis took the rifle and adjusted the scope while a COO-2310 selected the grenades. The J57-CM floated in, buzzing in droidspeak and broadcasting an image of what it had recorded on its telescopic lenses: the constable was near the northern ridge. Time was short.

An EG-6 gonk droid moved around the small

droid encampment, offering power to any who needed it.

CZ-1G5 stared at the blaster he was holding in his stiff white hand. Anyone who knew the droid well would have thought he looked . . . sad.

THE TRAIL had been easy to spot. Few speeders traveled along the southern route those days. The speeder's repulsor engines left a distinct pattern in the loose sands below.

It was as if CZ had left a map.

Zuvio looked down the long road and saw the ruins of an old freighter. At one point it had been heavily converted into a home—a poor fool's attempt at a moisture farm. That was clearly a very long time before, and the crashed ship had been empty—abandoned—for some time.

CZ's trail led directly toward the shell of the tall makeshift farmstead. . . .

Too easy. Too easy for a smart droid like CZ.

The constable suddenly slammed on his speeder's brakes. As he did so, a rifle blast burst from the distant farmhouse, clipping the front of the speeder. A sniper shot. If Zuvio hadn't stopped . . .

But that hadn't been simple chance. Everything about it smelled wrong to the constable.

Zuvio rolled behind a rocky outcropping, dodging a second shot. The speeder was ruined. The sniper shot intended for the constable's chest had instead pierced the speeder's engine housing—and more, judging by the vent of green fire spewing from its chassis.

The speeder exploded. Shrapnel burst across the barren landscape. One small shard of metal ripped through Zuvio's sleeve, cutting deeply. Biting back the sudden pain, Zuvio flipped open his comlink. Jammed. No help was coming.

The constable raised his blaster as another sniper shot clipped the rock only centimeters from his head. That was three shots. . . .

Zuvio had his assailant at a disadvantage. He

knew the capabilities of each and every firearm taken from the Niima weapons locker. The weapon being used was a Czerka-93U hunting rifle, plus scope and targeting computer. The targeting system was an after-market add-on, and it had never worked quite right. It was fine if the weather was clear, but on a sandy world like Jakku . . .

And it chambered only four rounds, with a three-second pause for cartridge reload.

Zuvio scooped up a handful of dry sand and hurled it above the outcropping, into the zone where the rifle's computer would be attempting to lock on to a target. At the same time, he stood up and aimed his blaster. There was a good reason Zuvio had never replaced the cheap targeting system of the old rifle: the system worked poorly with his eyes. The Kyuzo had problems with short distances. But long distances?

Long distances he could see quite well.

A shot from the rifle sizzled past his head, just as Zuvio had expected. The computer would now compensate and lock on to Zuvio, but the rifle would need to reload—buying the constable just enough time to do what needed to be done.

The constable squeezed off three quick shots. One would have been sufficient. He heard a loud metallic squeal and saw a cascade of sparks burst from the roof of the old farmhouse. A direct hit.

Unexpectedly, there was a rising scream in droidspeak from his left, and Zuvio saw a floating cam droid retreating toward the abandoned moisture farm. He was being watched. And more . . . it wasn't just a matter of one rogue droid anymore. He hadn't gotten a good enough look at the sniper to identify it, but it certainly wasn't CZ. So there were at least three rogue droids on the outskirts of town—armed and using lethal force. . . .

Zuvio didn't waste any more time in contemplation. He was a Kyuzo, a species that originated from a gravity-heavy world. That meant his muscles were more developed than those of the average bipedal species, and he could move fast when he needed to.

With a powerful leap, the constable covered half

the distance between the rocky outcropping and the farmhouse. Multiple blaster shots attempted to target him as he moved, but whoever was firing either hesitated or did not expect the speed the constable exhibited.

One more jump and Zuvio reached the edge of the farmhouse roof—a carbon-scored fighter shell of some kind. His large fingers dug in to the surface, and he kicked his way through a dilapidated makeshift window in the side of what was once a freighter docking port.

There were a lot more than three droids inside.

BACK IN NIIMA, unaware of the peril Zuvio was in, Drego and Streehn were examining the scene of the crime and interviewing witnesses.

"I saw him . . . I did," said an elderly female Ottegan, her elongated face bobbing up and down rapidly. "It was that droid . . . that CZ droid. He left the banking ship only minutes before the explosion."

"You saw him at the transport?" asked Streehn. "But you weren't in there when it exploded. . . ."

"And lucky that I wasn't!" she said. "I had an appointment with Mr. Lovas, but when the computer informed me he was absent, I decided to leave and do some shopping. Otherwise . . ."

The Ottegan shuddered and emitted a scared honking noise.

"It's all right. . . . Just one more thing . . ." Drego said in a soft voice. "What time was your appointment?"

A PARTICULARLY broken-down astromech designated B33 attempted to stun Zuvio with one of its attachments. The constable moved quickly, kicking the orange-and-green-striped droid backward into an ancient-looking RIC—a crude labor droid with a giant wheel instead of legs. To his left, a tall and thin droid that looked much like a stick protruding from a board, with half a dozen tiny arms attached—a WED Treadwell—flailed in robotic panic, and Zuvio shifted his attention to the much more dangerous DD-13 surgical unit. Balanced on its three legs, the tall, cylindrical droid lashed out with a scalpel, and

Zuvio barely had time to dodge. Again the blade descended, but that time the constable was too slow and he received a clean cut across the forearm in return for his momentary deficiency.

Meanwhile, the astromech was back for another attempt. The orange-and-green droid fired a tow clamp at Zuvio. Seeing his chance and vaulting to the right, the constable nimbly evaded the clamp, which then struck the DD-13. With a quick fluid motion, Zuvio shoved the astromech out the second-story window. Its metallic droid scream was cut short by a loud crash, and the surgical droid was yanked out the window as B33's tow cable automatically retracted.

In the background of the fight, CZ held his blaster. Despite his steady hand and fast speed, the droid wasn't firing.

The cam droid Zuvio had seen earlier slammed into the constable with a vengeful squeal. Zuvio shoved it to the side just as the Treadwell finally found its courage and rolled in for an attack. The multiple arms of the Treadwell were still flailing uncertainly, but even in a panic the droid's tool-arms could be dangerous.

Zuvio stepped backward, tripping into the melee. Amid the chaos, he heard the singsong chirping of an MSE droid. Zuvio knew that the Treadwell would choose that moment to strike, so he rolled to his side instinctively. There was an electronic shriek as the Treadwell inadvertently dispatched the MSE, which meant the heavily shielded MSE would send an ionic charge backward and deactivate the Treadwell.

From the corner of his eye, Zuvio saw CZ fleeing down the stairway in the corner of the room. Kicking aside the tangled mess that had been the Treadwell, he moved to pursue—and found himself blocked by an EG-6 power droid covered in grenades.

The constable paused. Power droids were encased in a durable shell, but if one were to be cracked open—which was very likely to happen there—the explosion would be . . . substantial.

Zuvio turned without a thought and hurled

himself out of the window he had entered through. The drop was not insignificant, and Zuvio hadn't had time to properly plan his trajectory. He landed with a robust crash, just as a deafening explosion ripped through the abandoned farmhouse. Debris rained all around him—both pieces of the homestead itself and metal shards that had once made up the now very broken droids.

Zuvio pulled himself up, bleeding and bruised, and he heard a sad whine coming from nearby. One of the rogue droids was still active.

It was the astromech—unsurprising. Droids like that were designed to take a beating. Still . . . the orange-and-green-striped unit had seen better days. One leg was torn off and the droid's chassis was ripped wide open. Its flat-top head clicked noisily, unnaturally, as it struggled to turn and look at the constable with its single, cracked eye.

That was when Zuvio noticed the restraining bolt.

BACK AT THE banking ship, Drego scanned the ID numbers entered into the terminal.

"Anything?" Streehn asked.

Drego shook his head. "Just standard transactions . . . until minutes before the explosion. You see here . . . ?" Drego pointed to the terminal. "All accounts were frozen automatically when the transfer occurred, but the explosion initiated emergency protocols on all communications systems, which includes credit authorization."

"And?"

"And then the accounts were emptied, everything in them . . . gone."

"To where?" Streehn asked.

"That's the thing . . ." Drego mused, tapping his thick finger on the monitor. "Nowhere. The money doesn't show up in another account. But . . . there's no trace of a transfer. None."

Streehn was frustrated. "Why would CZ rob the banking ship and not take the money? Why would CZ rob the ship at all? What's he going to buy?"

Drego folded his fingers in contemplation.

"I think there's someone who might be able to answer that."

THE SECRETARY DROID had left a trail of footprints through the desert sand, almost easier to follow than the speeder trail had been. Only this time, Zuvio was fairly certain he wasn't walking into a trap. No, CZ was panicking. His path zigged and zagged through the sands uncertainly. The droid was afraid.

Zuvio crested a plateau. The sun was slipping beneath the horizon, the desert stretching out into a wide plain of emptiness. Just a hard, rocky surface with nowhere left to hide.

CZ-1G5 was there, moving as fast as his stiff robotic legs would allow.

It was never going to be fast enough.

A wave of sadness washed over the constable; there was no way this would have a happy ending. No matter what had happened in the past day, CZ had been a fixture of the town for years—a part of the community in Niima. The bank transport robbery, the gang of droids waiting in ambush on the outskirts of town . . . Zuvio shook his head. It wasn't CZ. It wasn't in his nature. The droid just wasn't programmed that way.

But programming could be changed.

Regardless, CZ was a danger. If Zuvio didn't stop him, anything could happen. He had known CZ for years . . . but he was the constable, and he had a job to do.

Zuvio holstered his pistol and descended onto the plain.

"**I** DON'T UNDERSTAND. Why are you talking to me? That droid . . . that CZ unit . . . you should be out looking for him!"

The banker was in the constable's office, standing near the door impatiently.

"Could you just go over the timeline for us once more?" Drego asked, grabbing a datapad. "The details will help in the official report."

Lovas paced the floor, agitated.

"As I have already said, I know as much as you do! I was on my way to work when the explosion ripped the transport apart. When I got there, the damage was already done and you were on the scene!"

Lovas moved as if to leave. "Now if that is all, I have a considerable amount of work to do! I have to see about repairs! So—"

Streehn moved quietly, blocking the door.

"Thing is . . ." Drego continued. "Thing is, you weren't at the transport. We know that. But you did have a meeting. So why weren't you there?"

Lovas was sweating, fumbling nervously for his pockets. "A personal matter," the Kubaz muttered. "I had things . . . I had business. . . ."

"Business?" Drego challenged. "Business with who?"

Lovas looked up at the two Kyuzo deputies, glaring and angry, his long beak flushed red.

And in his pocket, the banker pushed a button on a tiny device.

"I SHOULD HAVE KNOWN. How long have you been wearing that restraining bolt?"

Zuvio's voice echoed across the empty desert. Knowing that running was no longer an option, CZ turned to face the constable.

"I'm sorry, sir. I cannot answer that question."

"Yeah," Zuvio said. "I kind of thought so."

The secretary droid's hand twitched.

"Since you probably can't say much, let me do the talking," Zuvio suggested, taking a cautious step forward. The droid and the constable were still far apart—more than ten meters. Odds were poor the constable could reach the droid before CZ raised his gun. Still . . .

"Those droids back at the old farmhouse," Zuvio continued. "I guess I'm supposed to think that was your gang? That you just turned bad after all these years?"

CZ paused. "That's certainly what has occurred. I have been a very bad droid."

"Have you?" Zuvio asked. "For how long? How long have you been bad?"

"I . . ." CZ hesitated as he searched his memory. "I have always been bad," he answered. "I am a bank robber," he added unconvincingly.

"Okay. Sure," the constable replied, taking another quiet step. "So where's the money?"

"The what?" CZ was getting agitated. That wasn't good. "The money is . . . the money from the banking vessel . . . it's . . . it's . . ."

Zuvio shook his head.

"You robbed a bank transport, but you don't know where the money is?"

Another step forward.

CZ was trembling. "Sir, I am afraid that I may be required to shoot you now."

The constable took another step forward. Still too far.

"Who put that restraining bolt on you?"

"I cannot answer that, sir. I am sorry."

"Okay . . . can you tell me who *didn't* put it on you?"

The droid paused. "I . . . I suppose . . ."

Zuvio took another step. "Was it me?"

"What? No, sir. Of course it was not."

"Was it either of my deputies?"

"Certainly not, sir. No."

"So it was someone else living on Jakku?"

The droid paused. "No . . . no, it wasn't anyone who lives on Jakku."

There it was, Zuvio thought.

Another step closer.

"Was it Rikard Lovas? Did he put the bolt on you?"

"I cannot answer that, sir."

Zuvio shook his head. "Sorry, Seezee. I think you just did."

The blaster began to twitch in the droid's hand.

Any moment it would rise, and the droid would pull the trigger. Zuvio gauged the distance. Too far. And the droid . . . Zuvio thought back to just that morning, when he had watched CZ file the papers in the office. The droid's speed was legendary. Maybe a trick he picked up long before, a quirk developed from never having had a memory wipe. Didn't matter . . .

CZ was fast. Zuvio felt a bead of sweat escape the war helmet he wore, but his eyes betrayed nothing of the fear or turmoil he felt.

CZ was fast, but Zuvio was a Kyuzo. He was fast, too.

The constable felt the grip of his small blaster in his hand.

"I don't want to do this, Seezee." Zuvio said. "No one else has to be hurt. Not me . . . and not you."

The sun was setting, the last of the light escaping.

A single shot was fired, and only one figure was left standing.

THE ORB-SHAPED DT-17 floated through the door into the constable's office, its laser turret glowing with a charge.

"You ask too many questions, Deputy," Lovas growled.

Streehn moved quickly, shoving Drego to the side and taking the attack droid's blaster charge in the shoulder. The Kyuzo deputy was hurled across the office.

Drego whipped his blaster from its holster. Too slow. The DT-17 fired again, striking him in the hand. Drego's gun exploded as it flew from his fingers—fingers he was lucky to still have.

"You couldn't just let the droid take the fall, could you?" Lovas reprimanded.

"No one would have known. No one would have cared that he wasn't guilty. The town would have had a villain to blame and the mayor would have refunded the stolen money. . . . No one would have known!"

Streehn tried to get up, slumping as he did so. Drego knew his cousin was hurt badly. Another shot like that . . .

As if sensing Drego's thoughts, the droid pointed its weapon at Streehn. Lovas smiled wickedly. "One more rogue droid. Two more bodies. I'll still win, and the both of you," the banker huffed, "won't be asking questions no more."

The DT-17 moved forward, preparing to shoot, when it suddenly exploded.

Constable Zuvio stood framed in the doorway, his blaster pistol trained on the banker, an inactive and blaster-scorched CZ on the ground behind him.

"That's okay," Zuvio said. "I think we've got all the answers we need right here."

S TREEHN FLEXED HIS ARM, noting the rapid healing. A small supply of bacta had been seized from Lovas's personal belongings. Zuvio had thought it only appropriate that the deputy get a touch of that before it was distributed to the other innocents injured in the attack on the banking transport. Nearby, Zuvio logged the last details on the case. The bank manager had been caught red-handed. CZ's data core had been examined by multiple technicians, and the evidence was clear: Lovas had reprogrammed the secretary droid to delete the record of all the credits in the banking transport computer, without actually withdrawing any of the funds. With everyone under the belief that the droid was the culprit and that he had transferred the funds to his own personal data core, the Kubaz would have been free to move the credits to an anonymous account at a later date while everyone was searching elsewhere.

It had been a terrible plan. Even if CZ hadn't been caught, eventually the accountants working for Niima's mayor would have found the money trail. But Lovas had been desperate. Seemed he owed gambling debts to the Irving Boys.

Difficult to pay those off while rotting in prison, Zuvio mused.

Handing the datapad off, Zuvio stood up and stretched. "Take care of this for me, will you, Seezee?"

The droid stood nearby, mostly repaired—inside and out. "Of course, sir. Right away," CZ said, his left eye twitching. The other eye had been destroyed in the standoff and was now roughly patched over with metal until a suitable replacement optical sensor could be found. Glancing at the data, CZ exclaimed, "Ah! Life without parole. I'm sorry to say that I cannot quite bring myself to feel badly for the scoundrel. Is that quite all right, sir?"

Drego stepped in, having just finished his rounds. Behind him rolled the orange-and-green astromech that had fallen out the window of the abandoned farmhouse. "Lovas got off easy if you ask me," Drego said. "Way too easy."

B33, purged of the banker's toxic programming, chirped and whistled in crude agreement with the deputy.

"Oh!" said a scandalized CZ, too embarrassed to translate the astromech's blunt droidspeak. "Well," he added, "I'm sure life in prison will suit him well enough. Come along, Bee-Thirty-Three. We have work to do."

So CZ and his new assistant embarked on their rounds to help the citizens of Niima, and Zuvio considered that at least just that once, on a planet filled with scavengers and pirates and thieves, the good guys had won.

Turned out there was something that felt better than a quiet day after all.

A RECIPE FOR DEATH

S HOVING HIS way past a startled serving and tasting BD-3000 droid, the sous chef known as Robbs Ely stomped down the hallway, away from the kitchens.

As usual, Robbs thought, no one understood what he was attempting to do. His food wasn't the kind of slop you could find in any kitchen. It was art. The methods he had learned during his long life while traveling from Coruscant all the way to the Outer Rim and back were unrivaled. Even Strono Tuggs, a.k.a. "Cookie," a.k.a. the head chef of Maz Kanata's castle and Robbs Ely's boss, couldn't match Robbs's skill with seasoning or sauce mixing. And as long as Robbs kept his recipe book private, it would stay that way.

Yes, Robbs had his own way of doing things. Ways that seemed odd or out of place in most kitchens, but that always yielded undeniable results. Did it matter that a dish had been ordered differently than what Ely concocted for the customer? The sous chef couldn't see how. All that mattered was that the food was good, and as a chef he knew better than the person ordering the meal.

And that's what the latest fight had been over. Cookie wanted the bantha meat buttered and roasted with a set of herbs that would make a Hutt gag. So Robbs had ignored the direction, followed his own muse, and created a dish fit for a prince. And what did he get for it? Kicked out of the kitchen! That's what!

Robbs Ely grumbled to himself and keyed in the entry code for his quarters. The door slid open, and from inside the dark room, a long blade appeared.

The sous chef never knew what hit him.

ROBBS ELY was dead all right.

    The Artiodac chef known as Strono Tuggs, nicknamed '"Cookie," stared into the deep freezer. Hanging inside, carefully and expertly butchered, was what was left of his sous chef.

    Cookie closed the freezer door with a heavy sigh. Old Robbs had always been difficult to work with, and his temper was legendary. It wasn't uncommon for the four-armed, orange-skinned Volpai to pick fights with other members of Maz Kanata's castle over food preparation, recipes, or plating techniques. In fact, just the night before, Robbs had unleashed that temper on Cookie himself. The pair had engaged in an epic yelling match that ended only when two of the scrubbers hauled the angry sous chef outside.

But that was just Robbs. Cookie hadn't even been offended. The pair had worked together for years, and old Robbs Ely . . . he was passionate about his art—something he and Cookie had always had in common. It had bonded the two in friendship easily, but as two culinary artists, they had been bound to fight over methods now and again.

"Not gonna be fighting anymore," murmured Cookie, an edge of sadness audible in his otherwise deep and grumbling voice.

The head chef of Maz Kanata's kitchens was tall; even with his hunchbacked frame, Cookie towered over most other residents of the castle. His stained brown apron hung low, almost covering his heavily booted and misshapen feet. And his head . . . well, it was never said that Cookie would take the lead in a beauty contest. Even among his own people, his asymmetrical features and wide flat nose left him a curious sight that intimidated or nauseated all who looked upon him.

It would have been easy for Cookie to descend into a life of resentment and dull anger. But that sort of path had never appealed to the misshapen Artiodac. No, instead Tuggs had always been obsessed with the art of food preparation. When he was young, he stumbled across some ancient holovids of a four-armed culinary genius named Gormaanda.

The experience had changed the young Artiodac, and before long he had dedicated his life to his newfound passion—cooking. That path had led him across the galaxy, from one end of the Outer Rim to another, always in search of the next great recipe, seeking the next best challenge.

The only thing that had ever stood in Cookie's way was his off-putting appearance. It overshadowed all he had labored to build, and no amount of skill or art in the kitchen could compensate—until he met Maz Kanata and was given a chance to run the kitchens of one of the most famous smugglers in the galaxy.

For over twenty years Cookie had served. For

over twenty years he had practiced and honed his craft. For over twenty years he had presented and created dishes of unexpected beauty and grace—as wonderful in flavor as the Artiodac was ugly.

It had been all the chef had ever wanted. And now it was at risk.

A body in the freezer—the locked freezer that only Strono Tuggs was supposed to have access to—expertly butchered in a way that only a skilled chef might manage . . . the body of someone who had been quarrelling with the chef just the night before.

It was a frame job, clear as day.

COOKIE DISPOSED of the body the only way he could think of. A quick trip to the dungeon, an unlocked cell or two, and one of the resident creatures would make short work of the remains. Any sign of the trespass would be overshadowed by the jailer's concerns over the escaped beast. The attempted frame would no longer stick. At the very least, the chef would buy himself enough time to figure out his next move.

Cookie didn't return to the kitchen right away, instead choosing to wander some of the less traveled halls of the large castle. Good for thinking . . .

And the chef had a lot to think about. Why would anyone want to frame him? Just to shift suspicion? Why not hide the body somewhere no one might ever find it? Riskier if caught, without a scapegoat. But still . . .

Cookie shook his head. Few beings in the castle could move about the place as freely as the chef. He was trusted—as trusted as any regular denizen of the castle might ever be. So maybe that had been the plan. Use the chef and his resources . . . force him into aiding the murderer, into eliminating all evidence of the crime—which meant the guilty party was accepting the risk of the chef's knowing about the crime, rather than trying to hide it completely.

Why do that? Why let anyone know? True, with the body landing right under his nose, the chef was in a bad spot. If he told anyone, Cookie knew he'd fall under suspicion. But he thought a killer who was smart enough to know that would also be smart enough to concoct a disposal method that would leave no witnesses whatsoever.

So the killer didn't just want to pin the crime on someone else. Cookie was being targeted specifically. And whoever put down old Robbs knew the way into the locked freezer, and managed to get in and out of the kitchens with a body without Cookie noticing.

And was an expert with a cleaver. Maybe as good as Cookie himself. So the guilty party had skills. Kitchen skills . . .

Cookie sighed. That line of thought wasn't getting him anywhere. Turning left down a hall, he headed toward the sous chef's quarters.

There wasn't much to see. The door was locked and only Robbs had known the code. Could be that Cookie could override it, but that would only alert castle security—not an ideal move at that point.

Something caught the chef's eye—greasy brown fingerprints on the keypad. Cookie hunched down and sniffed. A hint of sikoroot . . . a touch of cenwick . . . a few other herbs Cookie had never quite identified. It was the sauce Robbs had made the night before—the one for the bantha roast that had led to the fight. But the fingerprint . . . the Volpai sous chef had burned his fingerprints off a long time before. So these marks? They belonged to someone else.

The pattern and order of the fingerprints were easy to follow based on how much sauce was on each key. Following the pattern of the fingerprints, Cookie entered in the code, and the door opened with a light *swoosh*.

The small room was a wreck. Cookie had been inside before, and Robbs had been tidy to a fault. Someone had recently ransacked the place. And the safe where the old sous chef kept all his famous and controversial recipes? Unsurprisingly, empty.

The chef poked around the rest of the room. Not much to see at first glance. He bent down and pushed away some of the debris scattered on the floor. There were some slight scrapes on the ground. Thin lines, from a knife blade maybe? But too thin . . .

And there was one more thing. A small drop of blood—dried, though not for long. If there had been more blood spilled—and Cookie assumed there must have been—it had been expertly cleaned up. That one drop had probably been missed due to the wreckage strewn about the small room.

There was nothing else.

Cookie resumed his walk, heading back down the labyrinth of passageways. There hadn't been enough of the print for identification, he considered—too smudged. Other than solidifying the likely place of the murder, the scrapes on the ground didn't seem to tell him anything he didn't already know. And the theft of the recipe book . . .

It was enough to get the chef's wheels turning. The sauce . . . the unidentifiable spices . . .

"Problem, boss?"

Cookie looked up. In his wanderings he had naturally drifted along a familiar course and landed back at the entrance to the kitchens. It was early morning, and Cookie was surprised to realize he had been walking around the castle all night. Now his small team of prep cooks and scrubbers were on hand, preparing for the day's duties—a job that would be much more difficult with the absence of the sous chef. On top of everything,

Cookie would have to find someone to replace old Robbs. Someone who could match the skills of the sous chef . . .

A room full of eyes stared at the head chef. He abruptly realized he hadn't answered. "Naw . . ." Cookie said, looking at his underlings. "Naw . . . everything's good."

The eyes turned away, the kitchen staff resuming their various tasks.

Someone would have to be promoted. The role of sous chef came with purpose and prestige. It meant being a fixture in the castle and forever having a safe home serving food to someone Cookie considered one of the finest beings in the galaxy.

And that was it. Strono Tuggs, a.k.a. "Cookie," knew beyond a shadow of a doubt that someone in the room, someone in his employ, had to be the killer.

A FEW HOURS and a carefully concocted scheme later . . .

"So . . ." Cookie said to his assembled workforce. "Old Robbs has left us. Don't know where. Don't know why. Doesn't matter. But we need a new sous chef. So it's a lucky day for one of ya."

Cookie limped closer, surveying the lineup. "Here's the deal. You want the job, step forward now."

Four members of the kitchen staff stepped forward, leaving eight behind. The head chef smiled to himself. Two-thirds of the suspects eliminated, just like that.

"So here's how we're going to play this," Cookie said. "You grubs gonna compete. Each of you in four rounds cooking the best dishes you got. Last one standing gets the job. Understand?"

All four of the prep cooks nodded, shifting their eyes up and down the line and examining the competition. Cookie felt a chill. None of the individuals he was looking at had been working late night in the kitchen when Robbs was last seen. Any one of those louts could be the killer. Cookie stared at them, considering carefully what he knew about each.

The willowy Devaronian named Sama Macoy was new to the castle; she had worked in the kitchen for only a few months. She was talented, had a good sense of seasoning, and was certainly ambitious—but ambitious enough to kill?

Next was a Corellian known as Relva Jace. Relva was a brutish sort, sullen and angry with a heavy brow and long scraggly hair. He kept to himself, usually working in a corner cutting and dicing. He had some knife skills, that much was certain. But would Relva use those blades on a living being?

Damor Gregon was another human, with a shaved head and massive beard. He had worked in the background of the kitchen longer than anyone. Never fought. Never missed a day of work. Never got promoted. Had his long history of being passed over finally gotten to the prep cook?

Last was a Quarren/Mon Calamari hybrid named Jom Jarusch. Jom was a cynical sort, liked to make jokes about the futility of existence and was rumored to share whispers for a price. No one really liked Jom. No one really trusted Jom. But no one was ever likely to think the weasely amphibious creature was a killer. And wasn't that just what a killer would want?

Those questions would all be answered soon. One of the four had to be the killer. One of them had found a way into Robbs's private quarters. Maybe Robbs had walked in on the killer stealing his recipe book. Maybe killing Robbs had been the plan the whole time. But one of those four . . . They all had the knife skills. They all had the motive. None of them was working in the kitchens at the time of the murder.

One of them wanted the job of sous chef enough to kill for it. No way the killer would let that chance slip away by not using Robbs's recipe book.

Whoever was guilty would surely be incriminated through the cooking. The game was now afoot.

TO HELP give the ruse of a competition a ring of truth, Cookie drafted the two senior-most serving droids into the judging box. The droids, a pair of fairly archaic and heavily modified BD-3000 units, had long before been repro- grammed to analyze consumables for potential toxins through sensors built into the synthetic skin covering their right hands; their left hands were outfitted with a variety of utensils. Those upgrades, along with years of tasting experience, allowed the droids to conclude the overall quality and subtlety of a dish. More important, the serving droids were impartial in the matter and could be trusted to judge without bias.

The droids may have been upgraded internally with sophisticated analyzers, but externally they were showing their age. Their chassis were cracked and their once pleasing female-styled faceplates had decayed into grotesque parodies of humanoid features. Their legs and hip assemblies had long before been replaced with models far cruder than the carefully balanced gyroscopic swaying systems installed at inception.

The result was a pair of droids that were slightly attractive in some aspects, and yet horrifying to look at in others. They were, however, programmed to be incredibly diplomatic with sweet personalities.

Horrifying to look at was something that Cookie could relate to.

The head chef had converted his precious kitchen space into the ideal contest floor, crowded with every piece of cooking equipment he could find in the basement storage so as to accommodate the different competitors. Most of it was heavily outdated. Large double conveyor ovens and several massive mixing machines filled the room, along with some sturdy metal and wood tables. It was all bolted down—for safety. Long thick power conduits were strung up, hanging from the ceiling like ropes.

A couple of Industrial Automaton cam droids fluttered around the renovated kitchen, recording the event—and it *was* an event. That's how Cookie had sold the idea to the castle majordomo, as a competition to distract the sometimes unruly residents of the castle. It had been an easy sell; a storm was blowing into the region and there would be very little else to keep people entertained.

The judge's box was a large lifter platform designed for construction labor. It had been unused for some time but was sturdy and stable enough. It gave the three judges a clear view of the four-person kitchen below. Luckily the kitchen was currently in a space with a high ceiling—a holdover from when the room was used for storage.

The first challenge had already begun. Each contestant was tasked with the creation of a breakfast platter. The pantry had been stocked with all the supplies a talented and creative sous chef might need to make a stunning dish, and each contestant was permitted to bring a supply of complementary ingredients—to make it easier to figure out who was using Robbs's recipe book.

The aroma of grilled dianoga wafted up. Damor had carefully extracted the small amount of meat hidden in the upper back of the aquatic creature and was attempting to cook out the less favorable aspects.

"A risky venture," observed the BD-3000 on Cookie's left. That one was commonly known as Carly. She was the less broken down of the pair, and her face still held something of a pleasant demeanor—well, half of it did, anyway.

"If Damor overcooks the dianoga, it will activate the blood parasites that live in the fatty tissue. That will destroy the flavor."

"True," added the BD-3000 on Cookie's left. She was called J'Nell. Cookie had no idea why. Maybe it had something to do with her serial number. "But if Damor is successful, the dianoga will be a hard dish to beat."

Cookie shifted his focus to Jom. The amphibian was playing to his strengths. "I do not understand," said J'Nell in her pleasant mechanical raspy voice. "Jom Jarusch does not appear to be taking this competition very seriously. A dessert is not the best way to showcase one's talents."

The head chef grunted, narrowing his eyes as he answered the droid. "Baking is serious all right. No room for error. Jom messes it up, it's all over in round one." Cookie scrutinized Jom's methods. He was sifting what looked like basa root flour—distinct in its orange coloring.

"It'll be a spicy dessert," Cookie said. "You wait and see. That basa is no surprise. He'll have to work harder than that if he wants the job."

Pots clanked. Pans sizzled. The room was hot and filled with different flavors of smoke. It didn't bother Cookie. The air was heavy with the robust scents of his art—the art of food. And while someone in the room certainly had to be the killer, they were still all fine chefs.

A bell whistled and the cam bots drifted up around the judging box. Cookie pressed a button and the hydraulic platform slowly and loudly lowered to the floor of the competition kitchen.

Round one was over. It was time for the judging.

"TELL US about your dish," Cookie said to the first contestant.

Damor stepped forward, a wide grin hiding beneath his long and bushy beard. "What I done prepared for ya today . . . you see it's a pair of pikobi eggs, lightly basted and seasoned, with a side of flayed and grilled dianoga. It's a high-level dish, Chef. You'll see."

Cookie stared at the human. They had worked together for years. But could he be the killer?

"Tell me . . ." Cookie said casually as he cut into the dianoga. "Why do you deserve to be my new sous chef?"

"Well, with all respect, Chef, I been here longer.

I done worked harder. And I know food as good as the next. You make me the sous chef? I'll keep this kitchen in shape, I will. You'll see."

Cookie nodded. The food was good. The spices were subtle. The meat was cooked perfectly—no parasites!

Carly processed a sample, slicing it open with one of the knives built into her left hand and tasting the meat with a bare fingertip. "You have used two grams of fat for every third measure of water."

"Yeah . . ." Damor stammered, unsure how to answer the droid. "Yeah, I wanted to try and keep the meat from drying—"

"You could have achieved a better result with a pinch of grulluck oil. Cheaper and more flavorful."

"Well, maybe. But I hadn't much time and—"

"I agree with my counterpart," buzzed J'Nell. "You missed a perfect opportunity to elevate this dish. Next?"

"Now wait a minute—"

But Damor was cut off as Relva Jace pushed

past. "Shank of mousta, Chef. Sautéed and cooked rare, with a side of charred fruit."

Cookie sliced into the meat. It was particularly pungent, which was good. But the sear was off. And . . .

"Your seasoning skills are clumsy, Relva Jace," said J'Nell. "You know what is missing here, don't you?"

"I guess . . . I guess I needed more salt?"

"You *guess*?" interjected Carly as the droid cut her own piece of meat with one of her thin built-in utensils. "You know this dish is lacking, but you present it before us now as if it should win you accolades. How do you explain this?"

"Time," Relva said, meeker than Cookie had ever seen him. "I just needed more time. I got caught up—"

"It's not all bad. A little bit more focus . . . you coulda had something grand," Cookie said, feeling a bit sympathetic. Yes, Relva's cooking had been subpar. Yes, he wasn't fit for the role of sous chef. But more important, he had proven one thing with his uninspired and underseasoned dish: he was not in possession of Robbs's recipe book. He wasn't the killer.

Next up was a spicy fruit tart from Jom Jarusch. The basa flour base was well handled. Surprisingly flavorful. Enough to keep the prep cook in the running and under suspicion.

And finally, a double toasted seallia sandwich with a heavy and sweet blood syrup by the always grinning Sama Macoy. It was good. Probably the best dish of the day.

So round one was over. Relva Jace was finished. But the dishes of the other three . . . any one of them could have been a play from the recipe book of Robbs Ely.

Time for round two.

"**T**HIS NEXT round will challenge your skill in preparing food under pressure," said Carly.

"Agreed," said J'Nell.

The remaining three contestants/suspects exchanged confused glances. "What they say is right," Cookie added. "You all better keep your heads down and make the dish of a lifetime while you're at it. You hear?"

And with that, the head chef of Maz Kanata's castle pressed a remote button and the multiple blasters that had been rigged into the walls started firing over the contestants' heads. The guns were old, locked into place long before the head chef had found his way to the castle. And when the large room had originally been renovated to accommodate cooking, Cookie took advantage of the opportunity and turned them into remote sentry turrets—easy enough now to take command of and use to add some energy to the proceedings. They couldn't actually hurt anyone—not the way they had been positioned. They were firing far too high. But that sense of security was easy to overlook, given the circumstances.

"Interesting," said Carly. "Both Jom and Damor seem to have experience working under tense conditions. See how they both know to belly crawl when they hear the high-pitched whine of the stun cascade rifle?"

"Yes," added J'Nell. "But the time away from the table is costing them. Take note that Sama Macoy is working through the stun blast and accepting the slower reaction time in favor of the continual prep time."

"Well . . ." said Cookie. "That technique won't be helpin' her in the long run. See what she's makin'? That's a Devaronian specialty—a kind of tangy soufflé. I seen it before. But you need to know your whisk times. You slow down too much . . ."

A loud explosion filled the room with smoke— and it wasn't one of the prebuilt hazards of the contest. Sama's soufflé batter was extremely volatile and had to be kept in constant motion. The stun pulse had taken its toll, and the Devaronian had let her batter blow up.

It was more smoke than anything. No one was hurt. But the added chaos would make things interesting, not to mention the fact that Sama would have to start a dish from scratch, all while suffering the sickening effects of low-level stun blast exposure.

Meanwhile, her two competitors were moving quickly. Damor was already plating, and Jom was adjusting the frequency of the oven. Looked like Jom was going extra ambitious and making a special side dish. Not necessary for the judging process, but the extra effort might pay off if it earned the amphibian the win.

Of course, Cookie reminded himself, there was a larger game at play.

The bell rang. The round was over, and the judges prepared to taste the food once more.

"**S**AMA?" ASKED COOKIE. "Tell me about your dish. Tell me why you should be my next sous chef."

The Devaronian's eyes flashed bright lavender—an indication of her aggressive mood. Her voice hissed from her grinning mouth of sharp teeth. "I make a classic dish—flash-fried zuchii with a tangy sauce. It's good. It's crunchy. . . ."

Cookie cut into the zuchii. "And why," he said, as he sampled a bite, "should you be the sous chef?"

"You got no one better," Sama said. "I know how to tame the flavors, not cower from responsibilities like these worms." As the Devaronian spoke, she gestured at the two competitors who stood behind her. "I can cook. I can create dishes never seen in this system before. You see what I can do—"

"I see that you failed to create your first dish, yes," interrupted Carly.

"And you have the nerve to bluster while forcing us to sample a last-minute replacement," J'Nell added. "So unprofessional."

"It wasn't my fault! The batter . . . it was a bad batch—"

"It is a poor chef who blames the ingredients." Carly waved away Sama Macoy. Cookie felt bad for the Devaronian. But judging by the inferior texture and flavor of what she had made, she definitely wasn't working from the recipe book of Robbs Ely.

So she was innocent and therefore out of the competition.

Only two remained. Damor served a fried siso-fish with a citrus salad. It was excellent, far beyond common cooking. The heavily bearded human chef had really sprung back from his stumble in the first round. Jom delivered a spicy living zelrey wyrm. A very ambitious and daring dish, expertly executed.

Cookie never would have thought either prep cook could have delivered such an excellent meal. It would be all the more impressive if one of them hadn't killed to acquire his skills.

"THIS IS THE final round," Cookie said. "You have offered up some fine cooking. Shame there isn't a promotion for both of you."

Cookie stared at the two finalists. "I'm thinking, though, maybe we've been too easy on you? Maybe it's time to really test your skills. To that end . . ."

Cookie pressed a button on a small remote control in his apron, and the gravity of the kitchen abruptly cut out—it was one of the newer upgrades the chef had petitioned the majordomo of the castle for, a variable gravity floor grid to help maneuver large equipment. No problem for Cookie or the two taster droids, who were strapped in to the judge's box. But for the two competitors . . . ? As Damor lost his footing and scrambled midair, Jom used his long and slick tentacle-like fingertips to seek purchase on a nearby conduit.

And more, the ingredients that had been carefully scattered around the room also began to float.

The two contestants looked distressed, but Cookie only chuckled. "Better start grabbing whatever you can and get cooking. Yeah, you're cooking in zero g. It happens. Get on with it!"

It was definitely a sight worth seeing—and everyone in the castle who wanted to see it could. Aware of the plan, the cam bots weren't affected by the gravity shift, and they floated and flitted around, catching every comical angle of the two prep cooks trying to swim through the air after their wayward ingredients.

"Jom does seem to have the advantage," Carly said.

"Yes," agreed J'Nell. "His particular biology makes mobility an easier task. But will he turn his easier access to ingredients into an advantage, or will it cause him to overcomplicate his dish?"

It was true, Cookie noted. Due to the inherent elasticity of his somewhat sticky appendages, and his experience as an aquatic being moving in three-dimensional space, Jom was able to navigate the lack of gravity much more readily than his human opponent. Meanwhile, Damor was gathering several of the brightly colored fruits that had clumped together in the warmer current of air from the ovens. More than he needed, Cookie thought. Still . . . the human had delivered impeccable food so far.

Jom was making fast progress. The amphibian had managed to get ahold of a floating rack of baby bantha ribs. The cook was attempting to rub them with a butter sauce but was making a mess of the process. Drops of the sauce drifted across the room, floating through the air like bubbles.

Carly reached out with her sensor finger and dipped the tip of it into a bubble, tasting the

ingredients. "Intriguing flavors. Difficult to identify the spices. This being is one to watch."

J'Nell reached out and dabbed her sensor finger
into another nearby bubble. "Savory and sweet. A
bold choice to pair with roasted bantha. Indeed, I
believe you are correct."

Reaching out and tasting for himself, Cookie
had to agree. It *was* a bold choice. One that was as
unusual as the various herbs that had been cooked
into the butter. It was something that might win
the competition—but there wasn't really any reason
for the game to continue.

Jom Jarusch hadn't even tried to hide the recipe. It was the very same one Robbs Ely had cooked
only one night before. The last thing the sous chef
had ever prepared.

Jom was the killer.

COOKIE SLAMMED the button in his apron and reinitiated gravity ahead of schedule. A loud clattering rang through the room as pots and pans and utensils rained down on the floor. Unable to compensate for the gravitational shift quickly enough, the two cam bots fell abruptly, too, smashing to pieces. Cookie felt a twinge of remorse. Probably should have given some warning.

The two competing chefs also hit the ground hard, but Cookie didn't feel particularly regretful about that.

"What is the meaning of this interruption?" asked Carly. "The competition has not yet been finished. The round will have to be started over from the beginning."

"No need," Cookie replied. "Know all I need to know. You!" he yelled, pointing at Damor. "You got the job! Now get out of here!"

"But . . ." Damor said, glancing over at Jom. "But what about . . . ?"

Cookie had no patience for this. Damor could have been the guilty party he had been seeking, but Jom had practically signed the crime. Now the head chef had a killer to confront, and the "winner" of the contest was no longer a serious concern. "You want I should change my mind?" Cookie yelled. "Go!"

Confused, Damor scrambled to his feet and ran out of the room.

Jom was dazed, his scalp bleeding from the impact with the floor. In front of him was a large knife. Just to be on the safe side, Cookie stepped on the blade with his even larger foot, pinning it to the ground.

"What . . . what is this?" Jom managed.

"I think you got a pretty good idea. You think I wouldn't know what you did?"

Jom shifted his gaze to the ground. Seeing the knife under the chef's foot, he looked deflated. "I thought . . . I thought I could make a name for myself. Okay? I'm a good . . . I'm a good chef! I just needed some help. Some training . . . So I thought . . . I'll just borrow the book. Get some recipe tips. I still prepared the dishes! I didn't think—"

Cookie hauled the prep cook up by the throat. With his free hand, he reached inside Jom's tunic pocket and pulled out Robbs's recipe book. "You thought you could kill your way into the job! That's what you thought?" Cookie was beyond angry. *"You think stealing someone's recipe book's gonna make you as good as them?"*

"*Hk* . . . Dead?" Jom croaked in a confused voice. "Didn't . . . didn't kill . . ."

Jom's tentacle-like fingers were pulling at Cookie's massive hands. Didn't matter though. Those thin and flexible fingers the hybrid Quarren/

Mon Calamari had would never break Cookie's grip. They would never . . .

They would never leave fingerprints. They were too slick. Jom couldn't have left those marks on the keypad to Robbs's room. And he wasn't in the kitchens that night. He wasn't handling the sauce that Robbs made. In fact, none of the chefs were working that night; that was why Cookie had considered them. They were all unaccounted for when the murder occurred. But that would also mean none of them would have been in contact with the sauce that stained the keypad. . . . And the only other beings that would have touched the sauce—literally, they would have had to put their fingers in it—beings that left the kitchen area for long stretches of time . . .

. . . were the two tasting and serving droids.

Cookie's hand began to relax around Jom's throat. The prep cook was still alive. But where did the—

And that's when the heavy rolling pin smashed into the back of Strono Tuggs's head.

COOKIE HAD a thick skull—luckily.

His vision swam. He saw double. Triple. In front of him, a rusted metallic blur moved forward and struck down with a sharp motion. Cookie heard a scream. *Jom,* he thought. That was Jom. And the prep cook's attacker had to be one of the two tasting droids. But where was—

On instinct, the massive chef rolled to his left, narrowly dodging the strike of a thin blade. The razor-sharp edge cut into the stone floor, leaving a thin and deep cut in its wake. *Just like in Robbs's room,* Cookie thought. *How did I not notice . . . ?*

But there was no time for self-recrimination. His vision had mostly returned. Carly was towering over him. Cookie kicked with his strong foot and the droid fell. Grasping blindly, Cookie found a fallen frying pan. He turned, only just barely blocking a blade strike from J'Nell.

"Give us the book," Carly said as she picked herself off the floor.

"Give us the book and your death will be painless," added J'Nell.

Cookie stepped backward, almost tripping over Jom. Instinctively, the chef glanced down. Dead. Murdered by the taster droids. "You killed him," he said, unsure why he was even surprised.

"You should have just taken the fall," J'Nell responded. "You could have fled the castle. Left the planet. No one would have pursued you over such a small matter."

"Just give us the book," Carly said, her agitation growing stronger.

"Why?" asked Cookie. "Why is this recipe book so important? Why you gotta kill to get it?"

Carly slashed out with her blade. Cookie stumbled back, just barely dodging it. Instead, the razor-sharp knife cut through one of the power conduits connecting the ovens. Sparks showered the room, and a thick black smoke began drifting from the damaged ovens into the warm air.

J'Nell circled around the chef. "It is our primary function—to taste and analyze the output of the kitchens. To ensure the safety of those who consume the dishes served."

"How could we achieve this," Carly added, "when the sous chef insisted on using unknown foreign spices and potentially dangerous recipes?"

J'Nell moved in, stabbing. Cookie wasn't quick enough and the blades dug between his ribs—just a shallow wound, bleeding badly but he hoped not fatal.

Calculating her next cut, J'Nell spoke. "All we wanted to do was take the recipe book. Study it and add its contents to our database. Robbs Ely would never allow that. He gave us no choice!"

Cookie saw that Carly was getting too close. He swung the frying pan, temporarily stunning the droid.

J'Nell took advantage of the distraction and stabbed again, this time digging the blades deep into Cookie's shoulder.

"If he had just given us the book . . . No one ever had to die," Carly said.

"Yeah. But he didn't have it, did he?" Cookie replied between gasps of pain. He edged his way backward. He was in the heart of the makeshift kitchen. He pulled himself over some spilled baskets. "You killed him, but the book had already been stolen. You needed to flush out the thief as much as I did."

"We need that book," J'Nell said. "Without it, our database is incomplete."

"And once you are dead, there will be no more witnesses. No more problems," Carly added.

Cookie knew his time was running out. He grasped a heavy conduit hanging from the ceiling. It was the gas line feeding the large ovens. The chef tried to use it to haul his injured body over a heavy table, but the conduit snapped, releasing noxious gas into the already smoke-filled room.

No way out, Cookie thought. J'Nell and Carly both closed in. Cookie gripped the leg of the table with one hand. The two droids raised the thin blades that were a part of their arms.

Above their heads sparks flew and mixed with smoke. Equipment whose operation had been compromised by the broken cabling shuddered and screeched. The room was rapidly turning into a horrific landscape.

And then Cookie pressed the button on the remote hidden in his apron.

THE GRAVITY cut out instantly. Pots, pans, utensils, food, everything floated—including the two murderous droids.

Cookie looped one arm around the leg of a table that was bolted to the floor.

Carly and J'Nell were clearly outraged. "This will not save you!" shouted Carly as she floated toward the center of the room.

"We will kill you! We will have the recipe book and we will fulfill our primary programming!" screamed J'Nell, as she drifted lazily upwards.

The droids continued to yell and yell and yell. Whatever purpose they had once served had clearly been lost. Their memory circuits were corrupt beyond reason.

"Kill!" shouted J'Nell.

"Cut you! Slice you!" added Carly.

"No," said Cookie. "The game is over." And with that, Cookie reached into his pocket and pressed another button.

The weapons system activated at full strength.

In the air above Cookie, the weapons barrage began. Floating high, the two droids were caught in the crossfire. Cookie closed his eyes, trying to tune out the mechanical screams. The droids had served a long time. They hadn't always been killers, he tried to remember. But in his hand, he felt the hard cover of the recipe book of his lost friend, and he couldn't quite muster any real sympathy.

With one last shower of sparks, the power systems blew. There was a quick roar of fire as the gas that had been released ignited. And then the gravity kicked back on and the weapon fire stopped. And the two ruined husks that had been BD-3000 droids fell to the ground with a clatter.

It was over.

IT TURNED out luck was with Strono Tuggs. One of the cam bots hadn't quite been destroyed when it collided with the ground, and had somehow managed to capture footage of the entire sordid affair. There had been a bit of an inquiry, but by and large, castle security was content to see that the entire matter had been resolved with the destruction of the two taster droids.

Cookie was back at work in the kitchens. In front of him was a line of his prep cooks, led by Damor, the new sous chef.

"Okay then, grunts. Listen up," Cookie said, wincing only a little. He was healing, but bellowing still produced a twinge of pain. "We're a new kitchen today. We're gonna do some good work. And to remember those we lost, I got you all a copy of this."

Cookie started handing out carefully copied drafts of Robbs's cookbook. The time for secrets was over. Too much trouble had come from trying to keep things private. "You're all gonna study this," he said. "You're all gonna learn from it. This book? It's filled with art. The art of cooking. So learn it and live it." Cookie stared at his staff of cooks. His voice was deadly serious but held a trace of sadness. "I expect you all to honor old Robbs's memory. Understand?"

The room responded with a rousing, "Yes, Chef!" And then everyone went to work. There was a meal shift soon enough and no more time to play around. Cookie moved to his station and looked over the list of ingredients on order for the day. Some of them he was unfamiliar with. But that was to be expected. The new recipes were unique. And though the deceased sous chef had kept things secret when he was alive, Cookie knew that Robbs Ely would have wanted his innovations to live on.

Cookie had seen to that. He hadn't just made copies for his cooks; he had uploaded the entire recipe book to the Orto Culinary Academy. Even now, hundreds of new students were studying Robbs's work. And Cookie was certain that one day the old sous chef's name would be up there with the likes of great galactic chefs like Jlibbous of Zenn-La and Gormaanda the great.

There were worse notes to close out on, Cookie thought.

And with that, he got to work.

ALL **CREATURES**
GREAT AND SMALL

BOBBAJO MOVED slowly across the courtyard. Though in all fairness, no one had ever seen the long-necked and wizened member of the mysterious Nu-Cosian species move any quicker; it was entirely possible that the slow pace was actually a breakneck sprint for the ancient being many of the residents of Jakku knew either as the Storyteller or the Crittermonger.

Though Bobbajo had a patient and calm demeanor, the same could not be said for the many species of tiny creatures tucked away inside the giant stack of cages and baskets strapped to his back. The bottom cage was currently home to a dozen or more tiny gwerps—lean frog-like creatures with protruding tusks and horns. The middle stack of weathered wooden hutches carried pishnes, long-necked, soft-mouthed, generously feathered creatures that were an odd combination of avian and mollusk. Another cage was home to a solitary lonlan, a bulbous mammal of a sort that resembled a large, semi-inflated, mud-colored balloon. A smaller hutch, tucked away in between the many cages and boxes, was home to a mated pair of zhhee, a brilliantly colored and especially boisterous species of winged lizard. And at the very top was the grumpy-looking worrt named J'Rrosch that seemed to travel everywhere with the wizened old wanderer.

There were more, of course: several tiny cages tucked away here and there, populated by rare species that most on Jakku had never seen or heard of before and would likely never see or hear of again. Every time Bobbajo visited, it was common for him to carry with him a dozen or more indescribable creatures. And even if those animals were common elsewhere, on Jakku they were all rare wonders, each seemingly with its own story.

The town was called Reestkii—a word that, loosely translated into Basic, meant "the leftover." Reestkii was located near the equator of the desert world, and the only settlement on the planet worth noting—Niima Outpost—was over four hundred kilometers away. The town had no resources to mine, barely enough agriculture for the locals to survive, and not enough combined wealth to get passage on a ship to anywhere worth seeing—not that there were any ships other than the occasional bleak husk of something long before burned out. There were very few settlements of that sort— generally unknown or forgotten by the rest of the bleak world they were situated on. So any change in the dull and monotonous activities, such as a visit by Bobbajo, was well worth taking note of.

Reaching one of the long tables of recycled scrap situated in the courtyard of the small village, Bobbajo took a seat, hefting his cumbersome pack of animal cages around and setting it to rest on the bench next to him. As was usually the case when the wandering storyteller came to town, the locals slowly drifted toward him. It had been many planetary cycles since the Nu-Cosian had last visited, and people—especially the local children—were excited to see what Bobbajo had brought with him this time.

"Quite . . . a bit . . ." the Storyteller answered in his slow cadence. And with that simple statement, two yellow-bellied sand lizards darted out of his sleeve and alighted on the packed sand of the courtyard in unison. The lizards stopped as one, dramatically rearing back on their little hind legs and puffing their chests out wide. The lizards balanced in that position, swaying back and forth rhythmically and in tandem. It was a simple trick to the older residents of Reestkii—not that they understood how it was done, mind you, but they had seen it before. To the scattered children, it was absolute magic.

"But wait . . ." Bobbajo offered, holding up one

four-fingered hand. The lizards paused, turning back, and skittered toward the cage holding the pair of zhhee. Within seconds, the lizards had opened the cage, and the two zhhee slowly emerged. They lowered their feathered necks, and a lizard scrambled up onto each, gripping the back and neck of its avian mount tightly. Bobbajo began rapping his knuckles rhythmically on the table, and the two winged lizards began to dance in place, stepping forward and back, whirling, prancing—each in perfect time with the other.

The children gasped and cheered while the adults smiled. Unfortunately, it was then that the Storyteller's traveling creature show was brought to an abrupt end.

"Is that a ship?" asked one of the children, staring up into the bright sky of Jakku.

THE SHIP was a Zygerrian cruiser operated by a band of slavers well-known for attacking remote outposts on less-traveled worlds and kidnapping the citizens they found, commonly pressing their prisoners into work camps or selling them off to the highest bidders.

The ship came in quick, and there was no time for the people of Reestkii to muster any defenses—particularly as they had no defenses to speak of. Such things had never seemed necessary there, as there were no animal predators in the region and the local pirates and criminals were more likely to use their resources raiding holdings that actually had goods worth stealing.

The slavers descended. The people screamed and panicked and ran while Bobbajo calmly and quietly emptied his cages, releasing his many pets into the streets. The gwerps hopped away into the shadows of the buildings; the pishnes waddled under the tables, huddling together as they often did; while the lonlan bounced around casually, its body inflating and deflating over and over in an excited fashion.

J'Rrosch glared and hopped away to find some shade.

Soon they had all scattered. And just in time, as the long-eared catlike Zygerrians disembarked from the ship, laser whips and rifles ready to punish any resistance as they went about their dark business.

THERE WAS no resistance to be found. Suitably cowed, the unarmed residents of Reestkii were rounded up and forced into the large town hall building while the slavers pillaged the settlement for any supplies they could steal. There was little of note in the building. It was a functional but unadorned structure—four heavy stone walls with narrow slits for windows. The windows were high above ground level, impossible for any of the beings locked within to reach and peer out. Green and orange paint decorated the interior, but it was chipped and worn with age. There were tables inside and a handful of chairs. Otherwise, nothing.

"What will we do?" asked one of the citizens in a

panicked voice. He was Thaddeeus Marien, a bulb-headed Kitonak. And though his leather-skinned species was well-suited for the desert climate of Jakku, he was nevertheless perspiring.

Another citizen echoed that sentiment: "Slavers," said P'nll Vun, an amphibious Nautolan, shaking the thick set of dark tentacles that cascaded from his scalp. "What will happen to us? This can't . . . this can't be possible. The constable . . ."

A third voice cut in, this one belonging to Jol Bengim, a Chevin whose massive elephantine head stretched the length of his entire body. "I know their like. They'll take us and force us all into labor camps. I saw it before . . . back when I was on Vinsoth. We're doomed for sure. . . ."

All the while the children of the village stared nervously and silently, terrified at the strange intrusion into the peaceful and quiet world into which they had been born.

"Listen . . ." interrupted Bobbajo. "There is . . . yet hope. We are merely detained. Our fates . . . they are not determined."

Jol stamped his heavy hooflike feet back and forth impatiently. "Easy words to say, Storyteller. But words will not save us now! Nothing will save us!"

One of the children, a tiny hammer-headed Ottegan named Adlee, let out a minute sob. With a silencing glance at the emotional Chevin, Bobbajo turned his kindly face to the needs of the scared children.

"Children . . . listen. You will need . . . to trust in what I say. Help . . . is coming, and everything will be . . . fine."

The children sniffled and fidgeted.

"Let me tell you a story," Bobbajo began, gently beckoning to the children. They slowly gathered before him, forgetting their troubles—if only for the moment. "This story . . . begins with the tiniest of creatures . . . facing the greatest of enemies. . . ."

SMEEP—A TINY, six-legged mouselike mammal known as a thwip—skittered through the long air duct, panting from the heat. It was a taxing journey, but the thwip knew it would all be over soon. Smeep passed an open grate, her four tiny eyes noticing movement in the hallway below. There was a Wookiee in sight—a tall, fur-covered arboreal species from Kashyyyk. It wore a bandolier across its chest and was being escorted by two stormtroopers. It was an interesting sight, but it meant absolutely nothing to Smeep.

What was important was her mission.

The thwip reached a junction guarded by a tiny internal systems probe droid, no more than seven centimeters tall. The droid was a standard anti-espionage unit designed by Arakyd Industries. They floated throughout the air ducts, defending against intruders and reporting any unusual findings.

Smeep froze, but it was too late. The probe droid scanned the tiny, furry mammal, reporting its sensor findings back to the computer to which it answered. From there, a technician would review the data and see what had triggered the scan.

Luckily, the probe droid was designed to neutralize high-tech infiltrators, usually of the espionage class. It had no programming capable of handling a member of the rodent family, and with a lack of specific instructions, decided to continue its patrol.

Once the probe had sped away, the thwip continued on her journey. Smeep was close, very close. Three, maybe four more ducts and she would reach the paneling and the wires she needed to chew through. Then—

The sound of a barrage of blaster fire suddenly

thundered through the ducts. Somewhere nearby there was shooting and yelling. The thwip didn't care for that, both because her sensitive hearing was easily overwhelmed and because it meant she might be discovered before she completed her mission.

From below, a hail of sparks burned through the duct. Whatever was happening nearby was dangerous. Smeep ran. One duct . . . two ducts . . . a third, and then a left turn toward the next detention block, and down the narrow space between the outer walls, finally reaching the exposed wires . . .

More blaster fire. Smeep shuddered, hoping that whatever was happening didn't involve the adorably large Wookiee she had noticed earlier. She got to work chewing on the wires. First a red . . . then a blue . . . then another red . . . then—

Smeep jumped back as a spark erupted from the wires. Success. There was a hissing sound as a nearby door opened, and the thwip hurried back up to the duct and over to a nearby grate. Seeing

the cell door open, she dropped down and scur-
ried over to find her friend, the captive she had
sought to release from the clutches of the Empire
and its sinister Death Star—a wizened Nu-Cosian
named Bobbajo.

"WAIT A MINUTE," interrupted the skeptical Jol Bengim, the Chevin's gigantic lips flapping with disbelief. "The Death Star? Storyteller . . . of all the tall tales you have told, this one must be the tallest!"

P'nll Vun narrowed his beady black eyes. "I must admit . . . your story strains credulity. And even if you were there, how could you know what the thwip saw? How would it wander free while you were trapped in an Imperial holding cell?"

As Bobbajo raised one hand and opened his mouth to answer, a loud crash shook the building.

"Those cursed slavers . . ." muttered a shifty-eyed

human named Xavi Brightsun, his brow creased with anxiety.

One of the children, a human girl named Myette, frowned deeply. Engrossed in the story, she had completely forgotten about the perilous situation in which they found themselves.

Bobbajo looked about the room, sensing the deep fear and frustration in his audience. So, like any good storyteller, he continued to speak. . . .

BOBBAJO AMBLED slowly down the corridors of the Empire's notorious Death Star. His escape from the cell had been uneventful. It was as if the Death Star's security forces were tied up elsewhere. It was just as well, as the Nu-Cosian wanderer enjoyed the opportunity to search and explore the vast infrastructure of the massive battle station, particularly after spending so much time in a small cell.

Still, as much as there was to see, it wouldn't do to linger overly long.

Bobbajo reached into the large bag he was carrying. Like most of his belongings, it had been locked in the cellblock. Once freed, collecting his entourage of pets and friends had been a quick process.

Out of the bag flew a tiny snee named Qyp. And after a quick whisper from Bobbajo, the little creature darted away.

Qyp's little blue wings buzzed speedily as he darted through the Death Star's cavernous halls, searching for the correct terminal that would deactivate the tractor beam devices, Bobbajo's instructions fresh in his tiny mind. The Nu-Cosian had been quite clear: as long as the beams were active, the escape pods would be too hazardous for anyone to use.

A shout came from a nearby detachment of stormtroopers. They hadn't noticed the avian intruder, instead focusing their attention on a computer monitor that displayed detailed schematics of the Death Star's trash disposal systems. This was of no concern to Qyp; ignoring it, the winged snee flew onward.

The truth was, the tiny creature was immensely anxious and, as usual, skittish. All snees were well-known worriers; the planet they came from was so placid that they found just about any noise, or sudden activity, to be distressing.

But Qyp was an exceptionally brave snee, and he continued his search without much undue hesitation.

The long-beaked avian creature was no bigger than a human fist—and that included his wingspan—so Qyp easily flew above the sight lines of the many preoccupied Imperial agents who were running about. In fact, the only notice the snee drew at all was when he flew into a large office of some kind, seeking a clear path to the necessary terminals, and was spotted by an exceptionally nosy blue-and-green R3-L1 unit—which ended up being slightly problematic for Qyp.

The astromech chirped out an alarm in droid-speak. Qyp obviously did not speak droid and simply tried to pass the astromech, but it was plugged into the room's computer core; a quick twist of the droid's interface module and the doors were sealed. Qyp was trapped.

The snee grew more anxious than ever before. Bobbajo depended on him!

The droid whirled, disengaging from the computer system. The snee flitted about, seeking a new path, but there were none to be found. The astromech extended a prong, arcing a threatening burst of electricity at Qyp. The snee darted through the air, the lightning missing his wings by the slightest margin. Then came another burst of electricity and another narrow miss. He was brave for a snee, but even still, Qyp was scared—scared of the mean droid, scared of all the noise, scared of not reaching the tractor beam controls in time. . . .

But the astromech was unrelenting; its semitransparent domed head spun like mad, tracking the snee wherever he flew. Frustrated and alone, Qyp knew he had only one chance at defeating the evil Imperial droid.

Spying a small device mounted to the ceiling, the snee flew upward. The droid fired another volley of lightning—the blast striking exactly where Qyp had been only a split second before—and suddenly the device on the ceiling erupted, spraying water throughout the room. It was a fire control system, activated by the droid's attack.

The droid let out an angry screech as water rained down on it. Qyp flitted back and forth, mocking the mean-spirited droid, which was still advancing on the snee. The droid's entire body was drenched, and its wheeled legs splashed through the puddles that had formed on the floor. Qyp paused, a perfect target for the belligerent piece of machinery. . . .

The Imperial droid fired once more, and Qyp darted out of the way. The electric arc instead struck the water that was running off a console and onto the floor. . . .

The water carried the electrical current, sending it back to the angry droid. The R3 unit instantly began to shake, its many compartments and flaps bursting open from the overload of electricity. It made a single sad moaning noise as it fell over and landed on the wet floor with a mighty splash.

The winged snee landed on the nearby console,

tapping at the controls delicately, and the doors opened. On the other side was the trench leading to the tractor beam terminal.

Finally!

Qyp flew past two stormtroopers and overheard a discussion about reports and a drill of some kind. None of it made much sense, but they were distracted and that was good enough for the tiny creature. His wings were very tired after his battle with the R3 unit, and he definitely didn't want the attention of two fully armed stormtroopers.

Flying down a long hallway and around a corner into a large open area, Qyp found the tractor beam controls at last.

The snee landed and pecked at a couple of buttons. It was strange; the tractor beams were already deactivated—although the lock had been left in place. Qyp didn't really understand any of that, of course, but the little creature had well memorized the routine of instructions whispered by the calm and placid Bobbajo, and the snee could tell that most of the steps were already complete.

Most, but not all.

Pecking rapidly, the snee unlocked the automatic security field that would blast any ship escaping the Death Star with an automatic ion pulse. And with that, it was done. The escape pods, and any other ship, would be free to leave.

Qyp pitched back into the air, flying through the Death Star to escape with his friend Bobbajo.

BACK ON JAKKU, Bobbajo's recounting of the bold adventure was abruptly interrupted once more as Jol raised one of his enormous eyebrows. "A snee deactivated an Imperial tractor beam? I've seen your pets do marvelous things, I'll admit, but you know that's not possible!"

"Ahhh . . ." Bobbajo said slowly. "Qyp was quite clever. But even then . . . he did not deactivate the tractor beam. Instead . . . he simply unlocked the ionic disruptors . . . a task any snee might do . . . if properly trained."

"What happened then?" asked Adlee, thoroughly enraptured. A Wookiee child nodded his head and made a tiny growling noise, also wanting to hear more.

Just then there was a loud crash outside. Several of the citizens began crying in fear. P'nll and Thaddeeus exchanged anxious whispers with a large-eyed and hairless member of the Bith species called Arek Emjon, while Xavi Brightsun tried to climb up high enough to see out one of the town hall's windows.

"Are they coming for us now?" asked Myette, her eyes wide with fright.

"No . . ." answered Bobbajo reassuringly. "There is still . . . more story to tell. . . ."

NFORTUNATELY, an escaping freighter of some kind had placed the entire Death Star on high alert, and even with the tractor beam disabled it appeared to be an inopportune time to dodge the Imperial fleet.

Bobbajo pushed and poked at some controls he had found. The lights moved around quickly, and the panel made rude sounds, but eventually the Nu-Cosian was able to make a service door open.

The Death Star was like any place with lots and lots of people in it: there were janitor stations in every corridor. So the elderly Bobbajo stretched his shoulders, cracked his neck, yawned lazily, and sat down heavily on the single chair within the janitor's closet.

Pushing back the sleepiness he felt after such a long day of escaping an Imperial prison, Bobbajo reached down and searched for one of his cages. It was a little one, painted green and orange with a letter *M* engraved on its tiny door.

"Ahhh . . ." said Bobbajo. "There you are. . . ."

With a practiced twist of his wrist, Bobbajo opened the tiny cage, and Mideyean—a bright orange, thirty-centimeter-long limbless reptile called a slitherette—emerged. The tiny reptilian creature snaked around Bobbajo's arm, climbing all the way up to his face. The Nu-Cosian stroked the top of his tiny friend's head and with a little smile whispered a set of instructions. . . .

It was not long before Mideyean was alone, speeding through the narrow spaces underneath the Death Star's floor paneling. The panels were mostly solid, but every now and again there was a section fashioned as a form of grate, and the slitherette was hesitant to be seen by the Imperials.

And the Empire was certainly on high alert. Since she had left the confines of the janitor's closet and the company of Bobbajo, Mideyean had overheard many things—most of which revolved around a man in a brown robe having a sword fight with a man in a black cape, and a computer failure that had led to some kind of mass shutdown of all the garbage smashers on the station's detention level. The fight sounded bad, but more people seemed upset over the garbage smashers and the problems it had caused the sanitation systems. Explosions from garbage chutes had evidently been occurring on multiple levels, and the plumbing in the officers' quarters was overflowing from every drain.

The Death Star was a mess. But soon enough, the Empire's evil and oppressive forces would restore order to the chaotic battle station and return it to its sinister purpose—unless Mideyean fulfilled her mission.

The slitherette squeezed through a narrow crack, pressing herself almost flat in the process. There was little room for error down in that section of the Death Star, as the service pathways to the internal temperature systems were constructed in such a way that they would recede without notice. If Mideyean wasn't careful, she could find herself falling straight down through the service shafts to the core of the space station.

It had taken the snakelike creature over an hour to wriggle through the gaps in the wall of the storage closet where Bobbajo and his menagerie were hiding, and several more to reach the systems that would affect the local climate controls. The idea had been to keep the technicians and security forces working constantly so when the time came, no one would be monitoring the status of the ionic disruptor systems.

Mideyean was an independent creature though, and as she slithered through the station she learned a great many things, all of them quite fascinating to a small limbless reptile from a distant Outer Rim world.

And then she overheard something terrifying.

The Death Star was moving in on a moon of the planet Yavin and was going to blow up that moon and everyone on it.

Mideyean was hurrying to return to her hiding place; a new plan was clearly needed. Unfortunately, there was a small issue: Mideyean had been seen and was being pursued by a hostile and very deadly Arakyd internal systems probe droid.

The probe may have been only seven centimeters tall, but it still packed quite a punch; it fired a blaster bolt from one of its defensive ports, narrowly missing the slitherette. More surprising was that the blaster shot ricocheted within the enclosed space, back and forth off the floor paneling, and finally sizzled through a section of open grating. The interior of the space station's flooring was coated with a deflective surface, probably to protect against system malfunctions, but bouncing blaster fire from a security probe in an enclosed space while in a serious hurry? Things were about as bad as they could be, Mideyean thought.

"Hey . . . you see that?"

Mideyean shook her head. An Imperial storm-trooper had noticed the probe's blaster fire. Go figure . . . things had just gotten worse.

Suddenly, the compartment flooded with light as the floor panel above Mideyean slid open; the slitherette was exposed. A rough white-and-black armored hand reached down and grabbed her before she could escape.

"A snake?" the stormtrooper said to a nearby officer. "How . . . ?"

The black-uniformed officer sneered with disgust. "That's a slitherette. I heard reports of vermin from Maintenance earlier. Probably one of the labs. Best dispose of it quickly."

Mideyean tried to strike her captor, but his armor repelled her tiny fangs. Before she knew it, the trooper had dropped her down a disposal chute toward the trash compactors.

"**B**UT THAT'S TERRIBLE!" The voice did not come from one of the children. Instead it was the Chevin, Jol Bengim, who seemed most outraged over the treatment of the slitherette. "What kind of story is that? And what about the attack the Death Star was planning?"

The children all nodded their heads, equally engaged.

A series of thunderous explosions shook the entire building.

"What are they doing?" yelled Thaddeeus, terrified.

"They're going to bring the building down on

us!" shouted Arek, his shiny bald head glistening from fear.

"We will know . . . soon enough . . ." said Bobbajo, with a dismissive wave. "For now . . . let us finish the tale."

BOBBAJO CONSIDERED the time. Mideyean was overdue. With a long sigh, the elderly Nu-Cosian pulled Smeep and Qyp from their resting places and sent them out to search for the missing slitherette.

Tracing Mideyean's planned path hadn't been too difficult for Smeep, who knew the scent of Mideyean quite well, and soon the pair reached the open grate from which the stormtrooper had plucked the bright orange slitherette. Lucky for both Smeep and Qyp, the security droid was busy elsewhere, as were the Imperial agents who had captured Mideyean. Even more fortuitous, the nearby disposal hatch to the garbage chute was still in active mode, giving a pretty strong indication of what had happened to their friend.

Unfortunately, that was the end of the good news. The hatch was active but locked. And to make matters worse, the two animals could see their friend trapped at the bottom of the chute. Even more awful, the compactors were online, and the poor slitherette was in immediate danger of being squashed flat.

It appeared, to the great frustration of the two distressed creatures, that there was nothing they could do.

BOBBAJO PAUSED for only the briefest of moments as a series of shouts and screams echoed from beyond the walls of the makeshift prison. The clamor outside had shifted from concerning to confusing: something was happening and it made the citizens nervous. But before anyone could rise to try to find out what, Bobbajo raised a hand and continued his story.

"Mideyean knew she was . . . in trouble . . ." the Storyteller began.

MIDEYEAN KNEW she was in trouble, and it wasn't just that the walls were beginning to shudder and move in to squash her. No, it was something else, too. Something was in the compactor with her.

Something alive.

ANOTHER INTERRUPTION and one of the children shivered with fear. Bobbajo offered the child a warm smile, ignoring the fact that there was even more commotion outside: running, shouting, explosions. The sounds of a battle. Once again, Bobbajo nodded comfortingly to the children and continued his story.

"The entire Death Star . . . seemed to shake. . . ."

THE ENTIRE Death Star seemed to shake. It was as if a small group of fighters was bombing the surface of the space station. Lights flickered, sparks flew, and panels opened of their own accord—including the one in the trash compactor.

Qyp wasted no time, darting in and grabbing the terrified Mideyean moments before something massive and monstrous—a slimy creature with a single eye—rose from the wet depths of the compactor and tried to snatch the slitherette.

Returned to safety, Mideyean gasped for breath, conveying as best she could the danger the station posed to an innocent world.

The station shook again. Whatever was happening outside was getting quite serious.

Rushing back to the janitor's closet, the team of animals found Bobbajo waiting, his face showing not the slightest hint of concern.

"Well then . . ." the Nu-Cosian said. "I guess . . . we will have to blow up the Death Star then. Hmmm . . ."

There was a quick round of discussion, and within moments it was agreed: there was no time to wait and no reason to return to hiding. The plan to create chaos had to be shelved in favor of a new strategy: to jam the Death Star's main superlaser cannon and make it backfire. Luckily, the path to the cannon was nearby. The question was, could the animals reach the necessary systems in time to stop the planet-smashing superlaser from firing?

And as the great station rocked and shook from outside explosions, the three animals rushed to make the insides explode, as well.

THE LONG-FACED Chevin shook his giant head incredulously. "Wait a minute," he said. "I know this story! It's in all the history holos! The Battle of Yavin! But there is no way you were there or that these . . . these animals of yours—"

The bald Bith growled at the Chevin. "Let him tell the story," Arek said. "It's a good story!"

Bobbajo nodded to the Bith and continued speaking.

"Lucky . . . for the snee . . ."

LUCKY FOR the snee, the slitherette, and the thwip, the chaos of the space battle outside commanded all the attention of the interior patrols, and the three animals managed to reach the small maintenance shaft that housed the super-laser's firing mechanisms.

Unluckily, however, the relevant systems were far too large for any of the tiny animals, even working together, to disrupt. Something else was needed . . . something with offensive weaponry. Something . . .

Something exactly like the small but dangerous security probe droid advancing toward the animals right at that moment.

Mideyean moved quickly, striking the miniature

probe and wrapping herself around it. Qyp darted back and forth, presenting a target for the confused droid. It fired somewhat wildly, its aim thrown off by the squirming slitherette clutching it. The probe's errant lasers missed the snee but struck key points in the heavily bolted access panel, and it fell open with a clang. Smeep leaped inside and used all six of her feet to pry at the exposed cables, ripping them out with a shower of sparks. The crystal computer core that regulated energy input and output was suddenly vulnerable. Still clinging to the probe droid, Mideyean aimed it toward the core while the snee pecked at the droid's casing.

In a furious discharge of energy, the droid unleashed a full volley of blaster bolts at the thwip, but it was too late, as Smeep had already easily dodged the blasts. Instead, the blaster fire struck the crystal computer core, which instantly shattered and exploded with an energy that the three desperate animals were barely able to escape.

Climbing back to the corridors, the three creatures knew they had done all they could. The Death

Star's primary superlaser would no longer fire. Or more to the point, when it did, the entire station would explode.

It was definitely time to go.

BACK IN the makeshift prison, Bobbajo paused in his telling of the story. Outside the town hall where the citizens of Reestkii were being held captive, everything went abruptly quiet. No one noticed though. Everyone—children and adults alike—was listening to the Nu-Cosian's thrilling tale.

THE ANIMALS returned to the Death Star's storage closet, where Bobbajo had remained safely hidden. Calm as ever, the Nu-Cosian spoke in his usual slow voice. "You have been . . . busy . . . my friends," Bobbajo said. Qyp the snee bobbed and weaved excitedly in the air while Mideyean the slitherette coiled around Bobbajo's arm in a friendly greeting. Smeep the thwip stamped all six of her tiny feet excitedly.

"Ahhh . . ." mused Bobbajo, somehow—almost magically—knowing what they meant and understanding their story. "I see . . . I see. . . ." The Nu-Cosian stroked his long white beard. "Then perhaps we had best . . . leave this place."

Without too much more adventure or danger, the group traveled to the escape pod bay and launched themselves from the Death Star and into the depths of space. Through the pod's tiny window, they could see the great battle transpiring around them. TIE fighters and X-wings danced back and forth in a display of action and violence never before seen.

The pod blasted past another ship, a disk-shaped freighter—the same one that had escaped the Death Star earlier. It flew quickly past, failing to notice the jettisoned pod, and fired at a set of particularly nasty-looking TIE fighters flying through the space station's meridian trench.

Even from where they sat, Bobbajo and his tiny animal friends could see the distant glow of the Death Star's superlaser as it began to power up. It would happen soon.

Any moment now . . .

The firing sequence had begun. The Death Star was about to destroy a helpless planet. But deep within the space station, where no one could see, a small regulator failed to divert the deadly energy to its proper destination, and instead of vaporizing the planet below, the great gun misfired—turning its world-shattering weapon inward and ripping the Death Star apart. All that was left was a shower of glowing embers, quickly fading away into the darkness of space.

The evil that the Empire had constructed to terrorize the galaxy was no more, thanks to the invisible efforts of Bobbajo's tiny friends: the unsung heroes of Yavin.

WITH A TINY bow of his head, Bobbajo finished his impossible tale. The awe-struck children of Reestkii sat with their mouths agape and their eyes wide. After a moment of reverent silence, they jumped up and cheered.

The adult citizens moved in to have a quiet conversation with the Nu-Cosian. Jol Bengim was the first to speak. "Look . . . I appreciate you keeping the children calm. That was the right thing to do. And I admit . . . it was a good story. . . ." The Chevin spoke confidentially.

"But we all know that's not what happened!" interjected Xavi Brightsun. "The Death Star was destroyed by the Rebel Alliance! They blasted it through a vent with torpedoes! They had a Jedi and everything!"

Thaddeeus Marien paced the room, gesturing wildly. "And that was decades ago! It's ancient history! There's no way you could have been there!"

Bobbajo smiled. "History . . . is an interesting thing. We know only . . . the versions we are told. It does not mean . . . that there are not . . . other truths."

P'nll Vun shook his head. "It doesn't matter. It was a fun diversion but . . . there are no fabulous magical pets to save us. There's no story you can tell that will keep the slavers from taking us away."

Bobbajo shrugged at the Nautolan and began shuffling slowly toward the great doors of the main hall.

"Wait!" yelled Xavi Brightsun. "You can't go out there! You'll be killed!"

Bobbajo ignored the warning, ambling to the door and gently pushing it with one hand. The door swung open easily, and outside the pirates were . . .

Defeated. Or more specifically, beaten and unconscious. The citizens poured out of the town hall, shocked expressions on their faces. The cat-like slavers' vehicle was a smoldering ruin. A pair of slavers, barely visible, was buried under a pile of heavy crates that had previously been safely stacked. Another one slumped and fell from a rooftop, unconscious before hitting the ground.

It was over. The slavers were defeated, and the only apparent defenders that could have accomplished that . . . ?

Out from the wreckage and chaos of the slavers' defeat they came. The fluffy pishnes waddled up to Bobbajo and nuzzled his legs. The Nu-Cosian reached down and petted each of them. The gwerps hopped out of the shadows and bounced happily up Bobbajo's back while the bulbous lonlan drifted down to greet everyone, floating lazily in the breeze as it did in its semi-inflated form. One by one, the animals happily took their places in Bobbajo's crates, cages, and coops. Even J'Rrosch hopped out of the shadows, looking grumpier than ever.

The people of Reestkii searched all over their small village, but they could find no one else. Only more unconscious and defeated slavers . . .

. . . and the chests full of riches they had plundered from across the galaxy. Treasures that the citizens of Reestkii could claim for themselves.

As Bobbajo hoisted the elaborate arrangement of cages onto his back, the people of Reestkii stared in wonder at the Nu-Cosian and his menagerie.

"But . . . how . . . ?" said Thaddeeus. "They're just animals. And they . . . Did they . . . ?"

Jol Bengim's giant mouth opened and closed wordlessly in shock. P'nll Vun managed to speak. "It was all . . . everything you told us about the Death Star . . . But it was just a story. Right? Your animals . . . these animals . . . they couldn't do something like that. . . . Could they?"

"It was just a story . . ." P'nll repeated.

Bobbajo smiled. "Of course . . . it was," he said. "But stories . . . they are powerful things. Never . . . discount their . . . strength."

Then the Nu-Cosian began his leisurely amble out of the tiny town, in search of the next story to tell.

THE **FACE** OF **EVIL**

IT WAS a dark night on the world of Takodana as the lush, green forest-covered world was drenched in a storm of violent thunder and lightning. All across the surface of the planet, the many species that lived among the trees sought shelter, waiting out the tempest so they might return to their normal, mundane lives.

But in the highest tower of the castle of Maz Kanata, work was under way.

Thromba adjusted the vibro-scalpel, gently tracing the contours of the specimen's features. The cut was clean and even, despite the pointless struggling of the being strapped to the surgical platform.

Thromba chittered across the dark laboratory to her partner, Laparo. They were Frigosian, which meant they were short by galactic humanoid standards and covered in a thick layer of yellowish fur, with dome-shaped heads as wide as their shoulders. As members of a nocturnal species, Laparo and Thromba wore heavy black goggles to protect their sensitive eyes from the light. To compensate for the atmospheric difference between Takodana and their homeworld of Tansyl 5, rounded metal breathing apparatuses sat where their humanoid noses would likely be situated.

Laparo chittered back, removing her cybernetic black rubber arm and switching it out for one with a small circular saw attachment. She flexed her arm, and the saw began spinning, emitting a high-pitched whine as it did.

"Jibb!" Laparo said. *"Jibb jhu-woo!"*

"Jeeba!" Thromba said in agreement as she pulled a lever. White lightning leaped between the two imposing energy receptors positioned above the surgical platform, and then the color of the

lightning began to swirl from one to another in a striking—if disquieting—exhibit of the violently powerful technology at play. The creature strapped to the platform could not witness the spectacular display, nor could it see the vast wall of levers and switches at which the two Frigosians furiously worked—which was probably for the best, as it really was not the most comforting sight.

"Meep!" Laparo said in her high-pitched voice, her saw blade having reached its maximum speed.

And with that, the fluffy yellow Frigosian loomed over her subject and continued with the procedure.

MEANWHILE, in space . . .

"I'm sorry," the tall, red-haired, heavily tattooed female human known as Ryn Biggleston said, climbing aboard the single-person escape pod. "I know we go way back, and we've had some wonderful times together . . . but you're the only one who knows who I am."

On the floor of the V-13 spacehopper, BeeLee Amdas, a blond Balosar with wide blue eyes—eyes now tinged with betrayal—clutched at her own throat with one hand as a glass laced with poison slipped from the other.

"You . . . traitor," the Balosar coughed. "I'll see . . . see you burn. . . ."

BeeLee tried to drag herself toward the escape pod hatch where Biggleston stood. "Give me . . . my money . . ." she choked.

"My money now," Biggleston quipped, blasting the ship's control dash. And then, giving her former partner in crime a final kick in the head, she slammed the escape pod shut.

OUTSIDE THE castle of Maz Kanata, lightning struck and the wind howled.

The hunchbacked Snivvian known as Drix Gil clambered up the long winding stone staircase of the castle tower, his great snout flaring in irritation as his ample chops grimaced in an expression that many species mistakenly interpreted as a smile.

Drix had been tasked with seeing to the needs of the Frigosian scientists, and it seemed the two short and furry creatures were always requiring something: Equipment. Service droids. Energy. They had a constant series of demands, catered to by those within the castle with far greater influence and power than Drix held.

Drix entered the laboratory and was instantly greeted by a diminutive but enthusiastic Frigosian—Thromba, if the Snivvian recognized the cryptosurgeon correctly. *"Gubwanna!"* Thromba asserted in her shrill voice, jumping up and down. *"Geeb Wabla!"*

Laparo ran up to him carrying a substantial empty syringe. With another handful of screeching utterances, she shoved the syringe into Drix's waiting hands. The Snivvian teetered on the heels of his boots, barely maintaining his balance.

"You already have sample from Specimen Nine," Drix groused with exasperation. "Drix brought you sample of Specimen Nine yesterday."

Disgruntled, the Frigosian spun around in a circle, her arms extended horizontally from her sides.

"Gep Ghee b'wann?" Laparo squawked indignantly. *"Gep zhu!"*

"Hfff. Fine. Okay. Fine . . . fine." Drix molli-
fied her, rolling his eyes with irritation. "Drix get
you another! Fah!"

The Snivvian limped as he turned to descend
the long staircase and grumbled scornfully under
his breath as he carried the syringe down to the
basement dungeon.

Drix hated Specimen Nine. Specimen Nine was
a biter.

BEELEE WASN'T quite finished yet.

If she hadn't been dying from a deadly poison, she might have been impressed. Balosars were almost indistinguishable from humans save for two specific traits: two small sensory-enhancing antennae that protruded from the tops of their heads and an almost complete immunity to every known toxin in the galaxy.

Ryn Biggleston had clearly done her homework; BeeLee knew she wasn't going to last long.

Even worse, the ship was venting oxygen, and without a great deal of time—time BeeLee didn't have—repairs would be impossible.

The Balosar had worked with Biggleston for

ages, and in all those years BeeLee had never been foolish enough to trust her partner in crime; so she had taken steps against her inevitable betrayal. BeeLee might not survive, but she could certainly ensure that Biggleston's life would not be worth living.

With one arm, the Balosar dragged herself to the console and pressed a secret button hidden underneath the center array. BeeLee felt the light fading. There was very little time left to her—even if the ship weren't about to be consumed by the fire of an uncontrolled reentry into planetary atmosphere.

But even as the small ship began to burn apart in the gravitational pull of Takodana, the data core exposing every secret Ryn Biggleston carried was broadcast far and wide, to every government listening station in the sector.

"Revenge . . ." whispered BeeLee, with a cruel smile on her pale lips. "I always get my—"

The ship exploded, and the notorious criminal known as BeeLee Amdas was no more.

ON THE storm-torn world of Takodana, things weren't going well for Ryn Biggleston.

The escape pod had taken the criminal to the closest planet that she could reach without a security scan. The options had been limited, but it was worth it for Biggleston to stay off the grid until the heat cooled down. After all, she thought, no one knew who she was or what she looked like.

That was why she had needed to ditch BeeLee. The Balosar had been picked up by security cameras during the job on Nordis Prime, and her ID was now well-known, making her number seven on the Tashtor sector's most-wanted list. Sloppy but not unexpected, Biggleston thought. Amdas had been increasingly careless in recent months. An end to their partnership had become inevitable.

Besides, a full cut of the money sounded pretty sweet to the thief.

So Biggleston found herself on Takodana, a place where she hoped she could disappear for a while, until the galaxy forgot about the crimes she had pulled. Especially after they found the remains of her ex-partner drifting in space.

Unfortunately, that's not what ended up happening.

By the time Ryn Biggleston had found her way to one of the small outposts on the northern hemisphere of the planet, her face was blazoned across the holonet. She was a wanted fugitive with a bounty of 100,000 credits on her head.

"Somehow . . ." the thief whispered to herself, "somehow BeeLee did this. That treacherous little . . ."

Now every bounty hunter in the system would be looking for her.

Hiding on a lawless world wasn't enough anymore. Biggleston needed to disappear altogether. Lucky for her, she was on the right planet . . . if the stories she had heard were true.

Biggleston jumped onto a speeder she had stolen. The castle of Maz Kanata was close; she could be there before sunrise.

DRIX WAS beside himself.

Specimen Nine was gone. The lower dungeon cell was unlocked, the door to the caverns underneath wide open—and no one had been down that way since Drix had collected the sample the day before. He knew that as fact, because the key to the dungeons had never left his pocket.

"Yesterday . . ." his mind raced, trying to recollect what had occurred. "Yesterday. Drix unlocked dungeon door, unlocked cell door, collected specimen . . . dropped . . ."

He had dropped the syringe, he recalled. Dropped it and rushed to collect it and keep it from rolling away. Then he had left, locking the dungeon door behind him. But not the cell door. He had forgotten the cell door.

Drix felt his knees go weak. He slumped against the wall, the open cell door mocking him. Taunting him. Things were as bad as they might be.

The Frigosians were out of test subjects. The Frigosians hated being out of test subjects.

ONE NIGHT.

That was all Biggleston could negotiate. One night and she would be back in the wilderness—with no way off Takodana and a price on her head.

And to make matters worse, the storm was still raging outside.

The thief was in a large common hall within the castle. The room was filled with slablike tables and a scattering of heavy stone pillars and very little else. There was a variety of beings in the hall: a long-snouted Bravaisian was arguing with an Onodone. A robed Ottegan gently swayed in a corner, moving to the rhythm of the soft music that drifted through the lower corridors. There was even a group of small, bipedal ursine creatures—primitives by the look of them. How the beady-eyed, thick-furred, adorable bear-like creatures managed to find their way into a pirate den was beyond Biggleston. Though in truth, she didn't really care.

What she did care about was the complete lack of support she had managed to find there in Maz Kanata's castle. It was said that all were welcome— at least for a price. And just by glancing around the halls, Biggleston knew there were beings there with laundry lists of crimes greater than her own. But none of that mattered, a polite protocol unit had argued when she first arrived. The outlaw would not be accepted, would not be given more than the token courtesy all beings received for free: one night, no questions asked. Food, water, and shelter from the storm. After that Biggleston would have to depart or pay some very heavy fees.

And parting with her loot was not something the thief was prepared to do. That's why she had hidden her credits outside the castle walls, as well as stashing the speeder bike she had managed to steal from a nearby camp. Never knew when a quick getaway would be needed, after all.

Biggleston strode out of the common hall and down one of the castle's many corridors. She paused for a moment, taking in her environment. At every junction, a camera was installed, mounted directly to the stone walls, scanning and recording the presence of every passerby. As quickly as the idea of getting lost within the corridors had occurred to Biggleston, it was dismissed. Every step she took in that castle was being monitored.

Biggleston slammed her fist against a wall in frustration. Thanks to that double-crossing Balosar, she was as good as dead the minute she stepped outside the castle. Muttering a curse under her breath, the thief wished she could go back in time and poison her former partner all over again.

"Excuse poor Drix? But . . . you seem . . . troubled?"

Biggleston turned to find an earnest-looking Snivvian hunchback staring at her.

D RIX HAD been following the human thief
since she had first arrived.

The castle was small, and word spread
fast. Ryn Biggleston had betrayed her partner, a
Balosar criminal known as BeeLee Amdas. Amdas
had been around a long time, and she had made
many friends. Now someone with influence—one
of those friends—didn't want the traitor in the
castle.

Drix saw an opportunity.

The Frigosians were understandably upset at
having lost Specimen Nine; you could tell by the
way they flapped their black rubberized arm attachments and the yellowish fur that covered their

heads bristled. But the chance to make a considerable amount of money while performing delicate surgeries with a consenting patient? That was a golden opportunity.

The Frigosian cryptosurgeons might have been obsessed with their work, and they certainly were almost incomprehensible and somewhat creepy to most other species, but like anyone else, they still needed credits. Besides, the laboratory equipment the pair used did not come cheap.

"Greep!" said Laparo.

"Kikiki!" Thromba replied.

"What are they saying?" Biggleston asked the Snivvian who had taken her to the tower.

"What you want is easy enough." The Snivvian rubbed his hands together. "But facial reconstruction only gets you so far. . . . To reinvent yourself, you need to think fingerprints. Dental. Retinal. And tattoos . . . not good choice in your . . . uh . . . your line of work."

Outside, lightning flashed, filling the room

with an eerie radiance. Moments later, a heavy wave of thunder shook the castle floors.

Biggleston glared at the Snivvian. "How much?" she finally asked.

ONCE AGAIN, white lightning flared between the two energy receptors positioned above the surgical platform. Thromba removed her left arm attachment, replacing it with a syringe-based design that allowed the Frigosian to instantly mix, measure, and administer whatever chemical agent the circumstances required.

Meanwhile, Laparo adjusted dials and levers on the large control panel that sat against the far wall of the laboratory. The energy receptors surged in response, and the lightning arcing between them changed color rapidly, creating a dizzying rainbow effect that did not seem to trouble the two surgeons.

"Huu Zhee wubu!" yelled Laparo.

The Snivvian grunted, bending over as much as his awkward hunchbacked form would allow, and began turning a large wheel mounted to the lever array. In response, the platform to which Ryn Biggleston was strapped angled upward.

The thief was uncomfortable. Not because of the straps or the intimidating surgical procedure she was about to undergo—though, admittedly, that was a bit nerve-racking, too. No, she was concerned about something else.

The Frigosians had been quite insistent on one point: they would be the ones to determine how Biggleston would look at the end of the procedure. They were, as Drix explained, artists. And like most artists, the pair of cryptosurgeons had to find their muse and follow it as they went along. Every face, the Snivvian translated, was a story waiting to unfold, and the true story that was Biggleston would not be known until the Frigosians began exploring the skin, muscle, and bone of their subject.

They would guarantee a few things though:

Biggleston would still be human, or a reasonably close species anyway. She would still be female in appearance. She would look young, healthy, and attractive. To sweeten the pot, the Snivvian had arranged for a set of documents that would clear casual scrutiny. Good enough for Biggleston to get off-world and away from there. Once she was back somewhere civilized, such as Hosnian Prime or Candovant, she could commission a new ID, complete with a thorough background that would ensure the thief the fresh start she needed.

It was cheaper than safe harbor in the castle would be; still . . . it made her nervous, which was why she had refused to pay the full amount up front. She gave up a deposit out of the money she had kept on hand, but the rest . . . the rest of the money was hidden outside the castle. Biggleston had promised she would deliver it when the surgeries were completed.

It was hardly the first time Biggleston had lied to get what she wanted.

S O THE SURGERIES BEGAN.

Laparo preferred the more superficial and cosmetic aspects of her art—the delicate reassembling of muscle and the slight tinting of flesh. To affect this, the Frigosian attached an arm unit that functioned as a vibro-rotary of sorts. Then, when the muscles were properly adjusted to their new configuration, she switched to a needle arm attachment.

"Dee dee dee . . ." Laparo sang happily. *"Doot dee dee doo deet!"*

Laparo attached a plasteel mask over the newly reshaped facial muscles and nodded to Drix. The

Snivvian pulled a lever, and a specially altered gas discharged through the mask and onto the muscle.

Now it was time for the eyes.

Retina reshaping was possible, but it was far easier to simply replace the eyes with new ones. To that end, Laparo searched a drawer full of parts that the Snivvian had hauled up from the basement. There were several eyes to choose from: red, green, hexagonal, even multifaceted. But Laparo, knowing exactly what she wanted, dug deeper into the chilled compartment and retrieved a large pair of blue eyes. A bit larger than the originals, but that was something Thromba would account for when doing the bone restructuring.

In the meantime, Laparo turned her attention to the skin itself. First, the entire thing needed bleaching—tattoos everywhere! Once all traces of those markings had been removed, the Frigosian began the dyeing process. The skin was quite healthy despite the primitive ink applications Biggleston had subjected herself to; so other than the color changes, there seemed little alteration to make.

Hair color was easy—too easy, Laparo thought. Instead of just changing the color, she opted for a new texture. Only one would do for what the Frigosian had envisioned—thick blond hair, coarser than Biggleston's own fine red locks. Each strand needed to be implanted in the scalp, so Laparo attached a new device to her arm—one very much like a strange sewing needle—and got to work.

"Zwhee doo wha . . . zhua!" Laparo chirruped, bouncing up and down.

The Frigosian loved her job.

THROMBA EXAMINED the skeletal structure of the subject.

The first thing the cryptosurgeon noticed was a specific thinning of the bones, likely due to a period of malnutrition during childhood. Easily rectified, even if it was outside the order of the surgery.

Using her syringe arm attachment, Thromba injected a battery of chemicals into the bone tissue. It would take a little bit of time for the cells to respond to the treatment, so Thromba began some basic points of reassembly that met the needs of the subject.

For starters, Ryn Biggleston's new body would

be slightly shorter and her hips would be wider than her previous configuration. Both could be accomplished in one step: by adjusting the hip joints so they were constructed farther apart, five centimeters of height would be transferred to the width of the hips. Shortening the arms so the subject remained proportionate was trickier though. . . .

Thromba switched out her arm attachment for the circular saw. Sometimes the old-fashioned methods worked best.

"Ghu ghee!" The Frigosian called out. Drix hobbled over with the welding array. It was a large device that had cost the Frigosians a small fortune, but it was worth every credit. It could knit together bone as if it were welding metal—hence its name. Left like that, the bone would never be quite as strong as it had been; however, there was a means of compensation to be applied: Thromba added a plasteel sleeve over the weld. That would lend enough strength to the fused segment so it was as sturdy as the original bone.

Then there was the skull. That was delicate

work, because whatever Thromba did there, it had to complement the work of Laparo. Furthermore, proportion had to be maintained at all costs; that had been a condition of the contract with Biggleston, and the Frigosians had a reputation to maintain—one for quality work.

The cryptosurgeon first went to work on the eye sockets, measuring carefully against the eyeball size estimates that Laparo had provided. Wider and rounder. Simple enough. Then some slight altera- tions to the jawline and the nasal structure . . . modifications to the cheekbones . . .

It took some time, but finally the skull was ready.

"Dweep?" called out Thromba.

"Dwoop!" agreed Laparo.

So the surgeons, with the aid of their Snivvian assistant, began reassembling the newly shaped form of Ryn Biggleston, thief at large.

RYN BIGGLESTON couldn't sleep. The noise of the storm combined with the itching of her face conspired to keep the thief awake.

The bandages wrapped around her face were uncomfortable. Her entire body ached. Everything felt . . . different.

She was sitting on a cot in the back of the large laboratory where she had been placed after coming out of a three-day stint in a bacta tube. The extra time hiding out in the castle had been a bonus. That much more time for the bounty hunters to look for her elsewhere.

"*Shaboo shwa,*" said Laparo.

Drix Gil translated. "She say you can take

bandages off soon. When itching stops. If you had taken them off earlier . . ."

Laparo raised her black rubberized hand attachments to her own fur-covered face and made melodramatic melting gestures.

"Yeah," Biggleston muttered, grabbing the case her old clothes were in. Her new body felt strange, and her clothes no longer fit. Fortunately, the Snivvian had managed to dig up some loose garments for her. Unfortunately, they smelled a lot like Snivvian. "I get it. When itching stops."

Biggleston stepped toward the laboratory door. The hunchbacked Drix moved to block the thief's path.

"Now wait!" Drix said. "You owe. You pay."

"Yeah. Fine. When I see my face," Biggleston said, pushing past.

Laparo stepped backward, making a hissing sound and baring several rows of sharp teeth. Biggleston had seen a lot of strange things in the galaxy, but the giant, fluffy yellowish head of the goggle-wearing Frigosian exposing a previously unseen gargantuan mouth was definitely one of the stranger ones.

"Okay! Okay already," Biggleston griped at the angry Frigosian, who suddenly looked very much like she could swallow Biggleston whole. "Just hold on. . . ."

Ryn Biggleston was not an honest woman; she was not even an honorable thief. The idea from the start had been to skip the second half of the payment, get off Takodana, and say good-bye to the sorry mess that she had found herself in ever since BeeLee so rudely exposed her.

So it wasn't like she didn't have a plan.

Biggleston slipped her hand behind her back, grabbing a vibro-scalpel she had stolen while the cryptosurgeons and their hunchbacked assistant thought she was sleeping. She slashed at Drix's nearest limb, causing the Snivvian to stumble away in shock. That put her a good distance from Laparo, and the door was in reach. From there, she could make her way through the castle and escape before the alarm was sounded. The rest of her money and her stolen speeder were hidden in a rocky outcropping nearby, which meant soon Biggleston would be off Takodana and free from the wrath of the cryptosurgeons.

She wasn't quite ready for Thromba.

The other Frigosian had slipped into the lab quietly, watching the proceedings with interest. And when Biggleston attacked, Thromba already had her teeth exposed and ready to bite.

Which she did.

Ryn Biggleston screamed. The Frigosian's mouth was huge, and each tooth was like a tiny dagger in the delicate and newly reattached skin of the thief's shoulder. But Biggleston was no stranger to pain and shoved the short, fluffy snarling cryptosurgeon off of her and into a large table crowded with lab equipment.

Glass vials shattered. Steam and smoke billowed. A large panel of electronic equipment began sparking wildly. The lightning generators activated, cascading green and blue bolts at random.

Not one to waste an opportunity, Biggleston ran out the door and down the winding stairs.

DRIX PURSUED Biggleston as best he could, but between his injured arm and his natural limp, he was no match for the thief's speed and agility.

That said, Drix Gil knew something Biggleston did not: the door from the stairwell that led back into the castle was sealed. After all, it wasn't like the Frigosians had trusted the criminal; they had given the Snivvian clear instructions to lock . . .

Drix slowed to a halt, his hand shaking as he reached for his pocket.

"Oh, no . . ." he muttered to himself. "Drix did it again."

Drix pulled a key out of his pocket—the key to

the dungeon he had once again forgotten to lock. Even worse, this time he was almost certain he had locked the empty cell, but in his distress over finding Specimen Nine missing, he had failed to lock the door that led to the dungeons or to reseal the secret passageway that led to the surface of Takodana.

Drix ran as fast as he could. Maybe, he thought . . . maybe he could reach the door first.

BIGGLESTON DIDN'T HESITATE. When she saw that the door into the castle was sealed, she turned and descended farther down the stairs. It really didn't matter what was down there; it had to be better than going back up.

Her shoulder ached where the Frigosian crypto-surgeon had bitten her. She'd need to get that disinfected. Who knew what kind of bacteria the Frigosian harbored in that giant mouth she had kept hidden—

Biggleston ran directly into the Snivvian.

The pair fell down the remaining stairs, rolling into the dungeon with a loud crash. Drix slammed his head against the stone floor while the more agile Biggleston managed to avoid injury. The thief knew Drix was stronger—but he was wounded and disoriented. Biggleston didn't hesitate and struck her opponent's head hard and fast with an elbow.

The Snivvian wasn't quite ready to quit yet and countered with a punch in Biggleston's stomach that left her gasping. Soon the two were locked in combat, hands around each other's throats, both struggling for survival.

The thief soon won out.

"Stop . . ." Drix whispered, the voice gurgling out of him. "Stop . . . or my masters . . . my . . ."

And it was over. Biggleston knew she couldn't return upstairs, and she couldn't open the door to the castle. Probably too late to escape that way anyway. But then . . .

A flash of light filled the passageway, followed by the sound of thunder. Then a draft of cool, wet forest air drifted into the cell. There was an opening somewhere. Large enough to let in the light of the storm.

But there were no windows. Was there a way out?

There was. A small door that looked like part of the wall had been kicked open. Biggleston could not believe her luck. Everything was going better than she could have planned.

With that optimism at the forefront of her thoughts, Biggleston entered the passageway and sealed it shut behind her, believing that she had found the path to her salvation.

And in the darkness, something moved to follow her.

THE BANDAGES itched—especially two spots at the top of her head. Biggleston resisted scratching. The skin was rapidly healing under those bandages, and she didn't want to do anything to disrupt that. Soon though; the itching was declining, and she wouldn't have to wait long.

Feeling the passage walls with her hands and following the air current, Biggleston desperately hoped that the end of the passage was open and not a locked gate or, worse, just a series of welded bars without any chance of unlocking. The air current was strong, which was promising. And she was starting to think the narrow, cave-like corridors of the not-very-secret passage were starting to lighten. She could almost see . . .

. . . someone.

Steadying herself, Biggleston blinked. No one there. It hadn't looked like the Snivvian or one of the cryptosurgeons . . . but there were a lot of other beings residing in the main section of the castle. Maybe she imagined it, Biggleston thought. Maybe . . .

Suddenly, a slimy tentacle looped around the criminal's neck and Biggleston let out a surprised scream.

She instinctively kicked backward and made contact with something. An unnatural roar was the only response, and whatever was holding Biggleston hurled her down the corridor with significant force.

Biggleston struck the stone wall with her already injured shoulder, and the pain that lanced through her chest helped motivate her to move. The passage was definitely lighter now. It might not matter, she thought as she eyed the monstrosity the Frigosians had labeled "Specimen Nine."

In a flash of light from the storm outside, she could briefly make out the creature's appearance. Some aspects of the beast were recognizable: it had the three telltale eyes of a Gran, but its long mouth looked vaguely similar to the cone-like snout of the Kubaz, and those features were strangely out of place on the elongated, hammer-shaped head of the Ithorian.

There was more: horns on the side of the twisted-looking skull and a set of human eyes— very sad-looking human eyes—staring out from its chest. . . .

Biggleston gasped in horror. The body of the nightmare looked to belong to an Amani—a worker species from Maridun. Its moist tan skin was easily recognizable, as were the long, slithering tentacle-like arms the boneless creature had grabbed her with.

Reptilian, mammalian, planarian, amphibian . . . there were even some traits suggesting an insect-like race such as a winged Geonosian. And all those parts . . . they were mashed together like a reflection in a broken mirror. The being opened its long mouth, the tongue of yet another species lolling out of it, and screamed—whether in horror at its own existence or in rage at Biggleston's intrusion into its lair, the thief could not say.

Biggleston ran like she had never run before.

She heard the creature galloping after her. Biggleston felt its breath, hot and wet on her neck. The creature screamed again. It was earsplitting. Startled and in a near panic, Biggleston almost fell—but righted herself just in time. She knew that if she stumbled, she would die.

And suddenly she was outside in the night, the storm still raging. Biggleston didn't stop running; even though her lungs burned and every centimeter of her body hurt, she kept moving.

Finally, gasping for breath, Ryn Biggleston stumbled to a stop. Whatever had been chasing her had evidently given up; she wondered why.

No time to think about it now, not with the castle of Maz Kanata looming behind her. Biggleston moved fast as she could, running for the stone outcropping where her speeder and money were stashed.

Her money. Everything she had done . . . she had done it to keep her money. Money she had rightfully stolen. Money she had subjected herself to a house of horrors to keep.

Money that was no longer where she had left it.

Biggleston felt the panic rise in her chest. She had buried the money carefully under wet dirt and rocks. The rocks were gone and the dirt uneven from a recent disturbance.

She dropped to her knees, plunging her bandaged fingers into the soft ground. It wasn't possible. It couldn't be possible. Biggleston cursed under her breath. Everything she had worked for . . . everything she had sacrificed. Her friendship with BeeLee, her ship that she had scraped and starved for . . .

Her face . . .

It was useless. The money was gone. Ryn Biggleston stopped digging.

THE SPEEDER was still hidden in the deep bushes not far away; that much was working out for Biggleston. Pushing aside the shock and numbness she was feeling, the bandaged thief rode for the nearest town large enough to have a landing field but far enough away that she wouldn't feel watched by agents of the castle.

It took a solid day, but eventually Biggleston reached a suitable trading outpost. It was the first step toward a new life for the thief. She could steal more money. It would be hard to build her fortune back up, but she could do it. And she had a new face. A new body. No one knew who she was anymore. She was free.

And even the storm was fading, the moisture quickly being absorbed into the trees of the forest as if the long dark and furious tempest had never occurred.

Biggleston reached a commercial passenger ship. Small, but it would get the job done. Most of the itching had subsided, and there was no more time to wait. She had to take the bandages off. She had to get on board.

Biggleston quickly made her way up the gantry of the passenger ship, finding a secluded corner to sit in where she could forget about Takodana, forget about the Snivvian, forget about the crypto-surgeons, and especially, more than anything else, forget about the partner she had betrayed and left for dead.

It was time to look toward the future. It was time for Ryn Biggleston to find out what she looked like.

Unwrapping her face was liberating. Biggleston felt like she could breathe again after days of suffo-cating. The air felt strange on her skin . . . like the tingle after a limb has fallen asleep. It was almost like pain, but it was far too strange to be described as such.

Lifting up her hands, she stroked the contours of her nose and cheekbones. Less severe than they had been before . . . Her chin more heart-shaped . . . Her head . . . The top of it still felt funny in two spots. Like there was something under her hair . . . like small antennae . . .

"You, there," came a voice from behind Biggleston. It was a deputy. Most of those ports had constables and deputies. This one, a reddish-orange and very expressive Ubdurian, seemed to have a particularly nasty temperament. "Let's see some ID."

Biggleston turned, reaching for her forged papers. At once the Ubdurian brought his rifle to bear. "You!" the constable yelled, disarming the safety. "Down on the ground, thief! Now!"

"What? But I . . . I'm not . . ." Biggleston was confused. "How . . . my face . . . how could you know . . . ?"

Ryn Biggleston turned. Reflected in the

viewport window, she finally saw her new face for the first time. But it wasn't new. It wasn't a new face at all. It was softer, yes. And the eyes bright blue and larger than the ones she'd had before . . . It was very familiar, that face. Too familiar . . .

"No . . ." the thief whispered, clawing at her own skin. "NO!" she yelled, scratching more deeply.

None of it was right. None of it. That face in the window . . . it couldn't be her. She was dead. She was dead!

The Frigosians . . . they had kept their word. Biggleston was no longer number six on the Outer Rim's most-wanted list. No. Now . . . now she was number seven. Now she had a new face. . . . Biggleston clawed and scratched at her skin, eliciting sharp red streaks of pain. And somewhere behind that pain, the thief with a new face could hear herself laughing uncontrollably.

The Ubdurian blasted Biggleston with a stun shot before the thief could do herself any further harm. It didn't matter, Biggleston thought as she blacked out. That new face . . . it was worse than scars. It was worse than what she had witnessed in the caves.

The face of BeeLee Amdas. The face Biggleston had betrayed.

THE TWO Frigosians beeped happily at each other. Thromba and Laparo had just finished watching the holonews; the infamous killer known as BeeLee Amdas was apprehended trying to escape the town of Andui, thanks to a tip delivered by the Frigosians themselves. The bounty was not inconsiderable—especially when added to the credits they had found hidden in the rocks near the castle.

Biggleston had told them all her secrets while under anesthetic. Everything she knew and everything she had planned—including her intent to leave without paying. That was okay.

The Frigosians didn't really mind. Not as long as they were having so much fun. Which reminded them . . .

"*Dweep!*" said Thromba in a high-pitched voice.

"*Jhweep,*" agreed Laparo.

The cryptosurgeons returned to the surgical platform to examine the progress on Specimen Ten. It had been a long day and night of operating, but both fluffy yellow beings wanted to ensure that the process went smoothly. They were lacking in raw materials, after all, and they no longer had an assistant to help them.

The creature that had once been a Snivvian stared out from the bandages with mismatched eyes. Electricity arced across the sheet that covered its lumpy body. A strange gurgling sound issued from the vocal structure freshly implanted in the throat once belonging to Drix Gil, and the two Frigosians jumped around excitedly.

"*Gep Dowhoo!*" yelled Thromba, upon checking the vital signs of the creature. It lived! The experiments were a success.

"GEP DOWHOO!" Thromba yelled again, cackling maniacally as blue and orange lightning crackled across the laboratory.

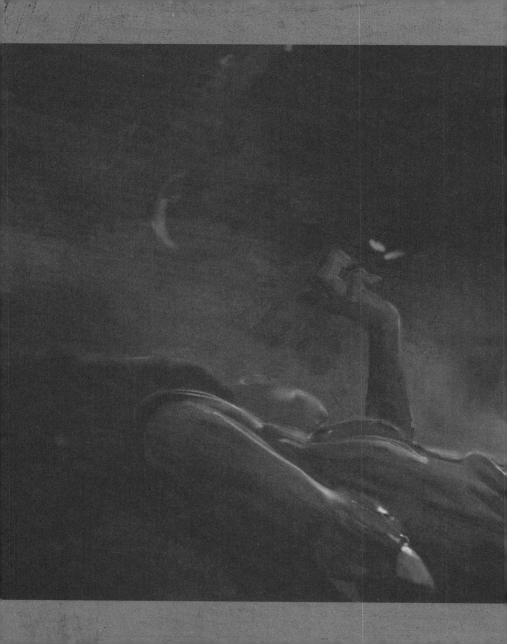

UNKAR PLUTT, the junk boss of Jakku, wasn't happy.

That was not particularly surprising. Unkar was never happy. At least not that anyone living on Jakku could remember. A large member of the Crolute species, Plutt was at home in a deep saltwater environment. Jakku, a dry desert world where water was one of the rarest of resources, was anything but comfortable for him. And for that reason, Unkar rarely left the security of his heavily armored headquarters: a converted cargo crawler that served as a sort of concession stand where the impoverished citizens of Jakku could take the scrap they had salvaged from the vast starship ruins that stretched across half the planet. They traded with Unkar for equipment, food rations, and most important, water.

No one controlled as much water as Unkar. And no one on the planet had any other wealth worth having. There were some stubborn holdouts who bartered their meager findings for off-world credits, and that small percentage exchanged their savings with an off-world banking company via a remote shuttle deposit/investment service. But Unkar had found a way to reach out and disrupt even that little bit of independence. A push here, a prod there, and next thing anyone knew, all those precious credits had been robbed right out of the shuttle. All without the junk boss having to get his own hands even a little dirty.

As for the rest of the population of Jakku— almost everyone—they had to trade what they found in the ship graveyards of the dry desert for life-supporting sustenance.

So they went to Unkar. And they begged and they borrowed and they cried and whined. As they should.

Unkar grunted to himself. They all wanted something from old Unkar. As if he ran a charity. Idiots.

The uncomfortably warm Crolute settled into the wide metal chair he had installed within his "concession stand" and looked out the window. It was a slow afternoon—unsurprising on an unusually hot day. With his large hands, Unkar activated a terminal and scrolled through a series of encrypted messages. It was part of his daily routine—not that there was ever anything in the messages other than the dry facts of his business transactions.

Delete. Reply. Save for later. Transfer credits. Withdraw credits. Delete. Reply.

Et cetera.

Every day was the same—which was just how Unkar Plutt would have liked it if he actually liked anything.

Which he did not.

"Boss?" a voice interrupted through the intercom. "Uh . . . hey, boss?"

Unkar glanced at a monitor. The screen was filthy and cracked, but it functioned well enough to broadcast images from one of the Crolute's many security cameras. The voice belonged to Scoggan, a thin blond human in Unkar's employ. Scoggan was, as usual, in the company of the much larger Trandoshan named Davjan Igo—which the large, orangish-green reptilian alien was fond of explaining meant "burning one" in his native tongue.

The two beings were too lazy to serve as scavengers and too cowardly to function as enforcers. But they were smart, and they were creative thinkers. And they served well enough as all-purpose minions.

It was one of those days when Unkar wondered why he even bothered. With a growl in his voice and a snarl on his droopy, corpulent face, the junk boss of Jakku answered his cronies.

"What are you doing here? You're supposed to be packing up the donations. Get back to work!"

"Well, yeah . . . it's just . . . you see . . ." stammered the clearly nervous human. "Me an' Igo here, we were thinking—"

"*Hsss!*" interjected Igo.

"Yeah," agreed Scoggan. "See . . . we were thinking maybe we could get an advance on our pay? Maybe a little bit of water to quench the, y'know . . . afternoon thirst?"

"That right?" asked Unkar, a dangerous hiss of his own filtering into his voice. "You think you gonna come to my door and beg me for a handout when I'm the one giving you a job?"

Scoggan turned pale. "Now wait. See . . . it was just an idea. Thought maybe we would work better if we were, y'know . . . ?"

The junk boss leaned into the microphone. The underlings couldn't see his face, but the tone of Unkar's voice was unmistakable.

"You get to work," Unkar said. "You get the

shipment packaged. And maybe, just maybe, you get half rations tonight. You get me?"

And with that, Unkar slammed off the comm and turned back to his monitor.

More messages. Messages that would normally have been answered by then. Back to work. The Crolute growled to himself. Back to what was important.

"**W**E SSSHOULD not have asked!" Igo hissed.

"You say that now!" Scoggan rolled his eyes at the Trandoshan. "But you wanted the water! You were all like, 'We deserve more water! Let's get more water!' Only with more . . . y'know . . . hissing and stuff."

"We ssshould not have asked!" Igo repeated. "We ssshould have taken!"

Unkar's two agents walked around the perimeter of Niima Outpost, giving a wide berth to the rusty shack the constable called an office. The law on Jakku was mostly focused on the comings and goings of ships, but one never knew when

Constable Zuvio might decide it was time to make a show of leaning on folks.

Scoggan was hidden under a thick layer of cloth and mesh, the only way to protect human skin from the sand and heat. The Trandoshan was less concerned. He was reptilian and thus more at home than most species in the harsh environment of Jakku.

"Yeah, you keep talking like that and see how long we're still breathing," Scoggan whispered under his wraps. "You don't just take from the boss. You even think it, he knows."

Igo waved away the human's concerns. "I think. I think many thingsss. We work like ssslaves for Unkar. We dessserve more!"

"Fine!" replied Scoggan. "More sounds great. I like more, too. But how? Everything Unkar's got, it's all locked up in his concession stand. And guess what, the guy almost never leaves!"

"*Hsss* . . . He has more. He has to have more," Igo hissed. "That old cargo hauler of his can't hold everything he's hoarded. We find his ssstash? We leave Jakku rich!"

"Yeah, yeah, yeah . . ." replied Scoggan. "Easy to say. But where's the stash? And even if we found it, you know Unkar. That stuff will be locked down somehow. We would need location, access codes, the works. You think Unkar is gonna just hand over that data?"

"I think maybe . . ." The Trandoshan smiled, his rows of razor-sharp teeth showing. "Maybe he would."

THE NEXT DAY.

It was hot again. Unkar could feel his flesh drooping even more than usual. The junk boss grunted. Hot. Just like every other day on Jakku.

And with that it was time to get to work. Unkar began scrolling through his messages, the same as every other day.

Delete. Reply. Flag for later. Delete. The same business. The same transactions. The same everything. Every single day.

Except . . .

One message stood out. It was a holofile. The source message was from . . . what?

A dating service?

Unkar didn't like when things were different. He felt a thin sheen of fresh perspiration spring out on his already glistening brow. What Unkar hated even more than new things were things he didn't understand. And he didn't understand why he had a message from a dating service.

The corpulent Crolute pressed the play button. A profile match, the holofile said. The somewhat corroded minicam built into Unkar's comm system made a shifting, grinding noise as it activated. It clearly suffered from years of disuse.

And then Unkar saw something he hadn't seen in years. A woman. A radiant female Crolute floating in the shallows of the salty sea of their homeworld.

She spoke. She said her name was Tanandra Frullich.

And she was beautiful.

SLOWLY, a new routine formed. Unkar was suspicious, of course, and he investigated the message heavily. It seemed that as an off-world member of his species—a species that rarely traveled off-world—his location and comm ID had been accessible through a public database. A database that the Everlasting Love Company (a subsidiary of ComGlom3k) purchased for exploitation rights in seventeen different systems. Unkar shrugged. He wasn't a young Crolute. He knew privacy laws weren't what they used to be in the days of the Old Republic.

So he responded to the strange yet alluring woman. She wrote back. And soon the two were engaged in a dialogue. The first one Unkar had held in years that didn't involve yelling or threatening someone.

Admittedly, he was a bit out of practice.

"So, yeah . . ." Unkar stammered into the holocam. "I left home after a . . . uh . . . business deal fell through. Drifted here and there. Finally found myself in the Western Reaches. Opportunity . . . you know?"

"I wish I could travel like you," Tanandra said. "I've never been farther than the third colony, and that was a moon! To be so far out in the galaxy . . . I bet it's beautiful!"

Unkar considered the barren wasteland that covered the majority of Jakku. He considered nearby worlds like Ponemah and Sahbrontee I that were similarly toxic and inhospitable. The Western Reaches seemed filled with the most backwater worlds anyone could ever imagine.

"Yeah," Unkar said. "Yeah, it's a real thing to see."

"Maybe someday . . ." Tanandra batted her

lashes. Her thick frame seemed light and alluring in the hologram. "Maybe someday I could come and see it? There's so little to do here on Crul and I've always thought of traveling . . . but never had a destination."

Unkar smiled.

Nearby, on a hacked feed routed to a makeshift portable transceiver, Scoggan and Igo watched, congratulating themselves on the successful execution of stage one of their plan.

IT HAD been way too easy. Igo had a background in comm repair, and Scoggan knew an Aqualish who used to program gaming interface systems before he became a scavenger. It cost a little bit in trade, but working for Unkar had some perks; most of the citizens of Niima Outpost were inclined to give favors to anyone with a little bit of power, and that was something Igo and Scoggan were all too happy to exploit.

Igo had come up with the plan. There were certain comm hacks—mostly useless on modern systems—that would collect personal data and extrapolate specific probabilities, such as passwords. More advanced versions of the system acted as viruses; they would piggyback in on another signal and infiltrate an existing database. There were limitations, but the more data you fed the virus, the more information it could derive from your files.

The original programmers of that viral tech were rumored to have been smugglers striking out against the Empire. Some believed it was a code used by the earliest incarnation of the old Rebellion, though it was impossible to say for sure. Whatever the true origin, the creators of the program understood that they could get more bites with the proper bait. To that end, the virus was programmed with an AI that, with certain tweaks, could customize itself based on the target. It would then function in an interactive capacity and prompt the target whenever necessary in its quest for data.

Long story short, there was no such being as Tanandra Frullich. Not in the evanescent oceans of the planet Crul. Not anywhere.

"**I** JUST DON'T know what to do!"

The voice belonged to Tanandra. And she was upset.

"My family . . . they found out I was in contact with you. And they're furious—threatening to cut off my comm system!"

Unkar grunted. "Is this because of the family you told me about? The Guhls?"

"Yes!" Tanandra replied. "I've been promised to the eldest son, a Crolute I've never even met!"

Tanandra's holographic image began to weep. "Oh, Unkar! I'm afraid I won't be able to visit your beautiful Jakku. I'm afraid I won't visit anywhere. Not ever!"

The transmission ended abruptly. Unkar slammed a fleshy fist onto the comm. Nothing. Tanandra had cut the signal.

But Unkar was in too deep to let things end so abruptly. He logged back into the matchmaking service and began typing the Crolute a message. *Tanandra . . . do not despair,* he wrote, far more eloquently than his rough voice would ever allow. *I have more wealth than anyone knows. I have influence with the Crolute government. I can bring you to me. I will not let this bond we are forging end without a fight.*

A moment later, Tanandra replied.

No, she wrote. *I won't let you bankrupt yourself. I won't let you promise money and favors you cannot afford, just for me. I will marry the Guhls's son.*

Listen. Unkar typed furiously. *I have means you cannot imagine, far beyond the meager stores I have described in my shop here.*

His fingers danced across the old comm board, almost gracefully. *There is great wealth in the ruins on Jakku, and I have exclusive scavenging rights. No one trades without my permission—which means the treasures of the old Empire are at my disposal.*

There was a pause. Then Tanandra responded.

What? What kind of wealth could there be in the ruins?

WEAPONS. FUEL. Rations. Water. You could find them all in the desert if you were crafty enough. If you were careful enough. The problem was, none of those resources aged well in the hot sun of Jakku. But there was something else . . . something present in almost every crashed ship on the planet. A hyperdrive system. Now, the hyperdrives themselves were usually beyond repair. But the interesting thing about hyperdrive technology was that it typically required a specific blend of metals to resist inter-dimensional shift stress—an alloy of titanium and chromium. Titanium by itself was junk, but chromium was quite valuable. Unfortunately, because the chromium in hyperdrive construction had been blended with titanium, it was, essentially, also junk.

Unless you had a very expensive machine that could melt down and separate the base elements—a machine that Unkar was telling Tanandra he possessed.

Don't worry, Tanandra, the Crolute typed. *You'll travel the stars and beyond. I have all this wealth . . . what use is it if I have no one to share it with?*

The holoprojector snapped back on. Tanandra looked stunned.

"You would do that? You would part with so much wealth, for me? Why?"

Unkar kneeled down, looking the small blue hologram of the female Crolute straight in the eyes. "Because . . . you . . . I never met anyone like you. Your smile . . . eyes . . . stories. I didn't know I was poor—poor in the heart. Not until meeting you." Within the comm system, the algorithm that was the entity calling itself Tanandra calculated and examined hundreds of points of data.

The machine Unkar described, when used to separate titanium and chromium, created a very specific gas byproduct, a low-level carcinogenic compound that was dispersed into the atmosphere. The machine needed a consistent power source, and it had to be located within a certain distance of Niima Outpost to be monitored, as any lag in signal could make a difference in the minute adjustments needed throughout the smelting process.

Then there was the matter of tracing the communication signals from Unkar's converted cargo crawler to the location of the smelter. That was the best way to determine which of Unkar's holdings contained the valuable ore. So far, Tanandra had detected that Unkar Plutt had over thirty-seven secret depositories scattered across the Jakku landscape. Any one of them could be the storage facility for the chromium smelter. To make matters worse, if Tanandra calculated incorrectly and her two controllers attempted to break into it, Unkar would figure out what the game was and shut it all down.

Nothing. Nothing that Tanandra had collected in her database could limit the number of possible locations below thirty-seven. All thirty-seven were equally viable.

It was starting to seem like a dead end. Tanandra was afraid she had failed in her primary mission—which meant she might soon find herself deleted by her controllers, a standard practice of those wanting to cover their tracks. That or they might reprogram her and try a new tactic. Either way, things were not looking good for the AI.

"I can see that you doubt me," Unkar said, clearly misinterpreting Tanandra's hesitation. "Let me show you my true wealth."

Tanandra was suddenly flooded with an upload of data. Pictures of a trove of the rare mineral, forged into perfect ingots. A ledger showing the exact transit dates for the unprocessed hyperdrives to the smelting location. Serial numbers of the loyal droids responsible for the operation. Enough information for the AI to easily extrapolate the location of the chromium.

It was an incredibly generous act of trust. One that Tanandra was programmed to betray.

The AI was just self-aware enough that she felt her first ever pang of guilt.

"**W**HAT ISSS the problem?" hissed Igo.

Scoggan and Igo were hunched over the makeshift comm receiver. It lacked the holoprojector of most similar devices, but that was a necessary trade-off for the third-party signal receiver they'd installed. At the moment, it was being put to good use for a secured and encrypted dialogue with Tanandra.

"I've analyzed the data. It's just that there are so many variables . . ." the program said weakly.

Scoggan scowled and pointed a finger at the terminal. "We got the signal! The system is designed to alert us when you've got the data you're looking for!"

Tanandra seemed to hesitate.

Igo pushed the human aside, his long reptilian fingers tapping the keyboard input rapidly. "Heh . . . I've sssseen it before. These AIssss get attached is all. They don't want to talk. But I'll get what we need. . . ."

"No!" Tanandra cried. Lights began flashing on the screen.

"She's trying to shut us out!" yelled Scoggan.

"No worriesss. We got this." Igo transmitted a code and suddenly the system went blank. A puff of smoke escaped from the main terminal.

"Aw, man . . ." whispered Scoggan. "You fried it."

"Jussst wait . . ." said the Trandoshan.

And suddenly the system rebooted. A string of information popped up on the display. Coordinates, security codes . . . everything. Everything the pair needed to rob Unkar Plutt blind.

TANANDRA KNEW there was only one thing she could do. She had to confess. To everything. Her programming no longer mattered, and most of her restraints had been ripped away when Igo overloaded the security protocols.

Unkar took the news quietly. It was not what the program had expected. She had expected bluster and shouting and smashing. While she had grown to love the Crolute, she knew his temper was . . . well . . . not quiet.

"Say something . . ." Tanandra begged. "Please, I love you. Don't turn your back on me."

Unkar squinted at the hologram. "You say this

to me? You work against me. You steal from me. You lie to me. And you say you love me?"

Unkar reached out and pressed a button on the comm system, shutting it off.

"No more lies." Those were the last words Tanandra heard Unkar Plutt say.

She called back. Again and again. But there was no answer.

IT HAD TAKEN Igo and Scoggan several hours to reach their destination: a mostly buried old Imperial transport. All but the large head-like cockpit of the massive machine was concealed under the shifting sand dunes of Jakku. Likely the canopy of the cockpit had been refitted with some limited field-generator tech that kept that portion of the old machine from being buried completely. That was an unusual expense and spoke volumes about the accuracy of the pilfered information.

Scoggan referred to the codes, activating a remote sequence on a very narrow frequency. Part of the transport's body emerged from the sand. A small hatch, possibly used for maintenance, opened near the top of the transport, pushing piles of hot sand off the giant vehicle in cascades. It was the entrance to the hidden wealth of Unkar.

Igo moved first, armed with a heavy staff, quietly hissing to himself as he searched the cavernous entrance.

"Anything?" asked Scoggan.

"It'sss clear," the Trandoshan responded. "The AI was right on the money. All the ssssecurity cams appear disabled."

Scoggan scrambled and skidded through the sand, then jumped into the transport's open hatch. "Let's not waste any time then," the human said. "Old Unkar is gonna figure out what we're up to eventually. We get this, we find transport out, we vanish somewhere in the Outer Rim."

Igo nodded curtly, and soon both beings were inside the transport. With a grinding shriek, the hatch slowly lowered, plunging them in darkness.

Scoggan hit the beams on his protective head gear and light flooded the compartment.

The transport was a relic, though in surprisingly

good shape. The space they stood in was large enough for several beings to maneuver comfortably, giving an indication that the entirety of the machine was almost too big to conceive of for a non-space-faring vehicle.

"I heard of these," Scoggan said. "Imperial armored transports. Giant four-legged things that were used to keep the peace on conquered worlds."

"Ssso?" Igo shrugged, following the human through a doorway and down a corridor. "That was long ago. Not important."

"It is if we want to navigate. These things were built sturdy and had a lot of internal security. Unkar is sure to have taken advantage of—"

And that's when a door behind the pair slid shut, cutting off the path to the surface.

"**R**ELAX," SCOGGAN SAID. "It's an automated system. No one knows we're here."

"Won't do usssss much good if we're trapped."

"I said relax. . . ." Scoggan patted the remote override they had programmed with the codes acquired from Tanandra. "We're in control here. We got the keys. Now let's go get those riches."

In a far corner, a small security camera clicked and whirred, almost imperceptibly. Tanandra was watching everything. And bit by bit, she was overriding the system.

She would show Unkar that she hadn't betrayed him. Not really. She'd earn his love back.

Deeper and deeper Igo and Scoggan descended into the buried transport. And with each step they took, Tanandra asserted more and more control.

THE INTERIOR of the transport had been picked over. Anything of value was long gone. But the two thieves were still on the upper level. The schematics they had acquired suggested that the actual processing machinery and storage for the chromium were below.

But the hatch was nowhere to be found.

"How is this posssssible?" asked Igo, scowling.

"The original hatch must have been sealed over," Scoggan said as he crawled around on his hands and knees, searching for the passage to the lower level. "Check the walls. Maybe there's a service conduit or—"

That was when the camouflaged vent tube opened and both Igo and Scoggan fell into the long shaft and slid quickly and painfully to the next level.

"**I** THOUGHT YOU were in control of the sssystem!" Igo shouted.

"I am!" Scoggan shouted back as he lifted his bruised body off the metal floor. "The override is just running a bit glitchy. Here . . ."

The human rapidly pressed a button. A light flashed on.

Igo and Scoggan were standing in the middle of a wide room. It was empty, save for a single door. Next to the door was a keypad.

Scoggan sauntered confidently over to the keypad. "See, this is exactly where we're supposed to be! On the other side of that door—"

An electric shock burst from the panel, hitting Scoggan and sending him flying backward.

Igo shook his head. "You should just stop talking. Every time you open that mouth, something bad happens."

Scoggan shook his head, sitting up. His blond hair was standing straight up and he looked dazed. "Are we in?" he asked.

Igo let out a sigh of exasperation and walked across the room. Instead of reaching out and touching the panel, the Trandoshan slammed it with the butt of his heavy staff, sending a shower of sparks into the room.

The door opened.

And in the background, a frustrated Tanandra watched.

BEYOND THE DOOR, there was a short, narrow hallway, and then another door. Igo stepped toward it impatiently. Scoggan grabbed him by the collar and yanked him back just as a cascade of blaster fire erupted through the narrow passage.

"Not so fast," Scoggan warned.

"You said the sssystems were deactivated!" Igo yelled.

"They were! And now they're coming on again!" Scoggan shook his head. "Just give me a minute. I planned for this."

The human took a metallic orb out of his pocket and threw it toward the door on the far end.

"A denton?" Igo looked panicked. "You crazy—"

The small explosive device went off. But instead of a cascade of concussive fire, it released a heavy pulse of ionic energy that disrupted the guns.

Tanandra felt her core being torn apart, and for a moment she was nothing. Then she rebooted and was self-aware again.

And she was also aware that her program no longer had access to the Imperial transport.

"THOUGHT YOU could pull one over on us? Eh?"

Scoggan was peering at Tanandra through a small camera. She realized with a start that she had been stripped of most of her primary functions and transferred into a low-memory, low-processor system—a wrist comm? Yes, she realized after a brief diagnostic.

The comm was one of the more modern varieties. It included its own limited holoprojector. Tanandra could see her captors—Igo and Scoggan. And they could see her. She was vulnerable. Helpless.

"Yeah . . ." Scoggan started with a sneer. "You think you're so—"

A heavy reptilian arm slammed into Scoggan's

torso. It was Igo, and he looked angry. He was likely about to threaten the AI with deletion or gloat about having found the ingots. Tanandra knew she had failed to redeem herself. She could never return to Unkar—even if she somehow escaped certain destruction at the hands of her controllers.

But Igo said something unexpected. "Where'sss the chromium? You said it was here! Right here!"

Tanandra blinked. She tried to run a data check, but she was partitioned off from the sensors. The wrist comm was really a prison—nothing more.

"It's . . . it's supposed to be here," she stammered. "It's . . . but Unkar said. He showed me . . . he told me . . . he . . ."

"Lied," a voice interrupted. "I think that's the word you're looking for."

The voice was distorted, coming through a loudspeaker. But it was still unmistakable. It belonged to Unkar Plutt. The Crolute had left his concession stand and was standing only five meters away, behind a thick slab of reinforced transparisteel.

And he was grinning.

"OH, NO . . ." muttered Scoggan.

"Darling," whispered the small holographic projection of Tanandra. "I don't understand. . . ."

"Yeah," Unkar said with a cruel laugh. "You probably wouldn't." The junk boss of Jakku stared at his two former employees. "Which one of you was it? Which one of you thought up the details of this little scheme?"

"Ah . . ." said Igo.

"It was him!" yelled Scoggan.

"Doesn't matter," Unkar said. "It's just that, in all your planning and programming, you missed one small detail."

"Impossible!" shouted Igo. "The AI was perfectly tailored to your interests! Everything . . . every part of our plan was perfect!"

"You sent a holo of a female Crolute," Unkar replied. "No such thing. Crolutes are exclusively male. The Gilliands on my planet—they're the female ones. Shoulda tried one of them."

"Oh," said Igo, his bravado now fled.

"So . . ." ventured Scoggan. "Would that have worked?"

"Not a chance." Unkar grinned. "You missed something else. I already have a love. And it's called money."

And with that, Tanandra felt her metaphorical heart shatter.

UNKAR PRESSED a few buttons on the other side of the unbreakable window. "The moment I saw that first message, I knew someone was up to something. Just didn't know who."

The lights flickered. Unkar's fleshy fingers moved quickly.

"I played along. Gave you what you thought you wanted. Steered you where I wanted you steered. You like this place?"

"Not a lot, no," Scoggan admitted.

"Where are the chromium ingots?" asked Igo.

"Look at you." Unkar laughed. "Stubborn. I like that. But you should have realized by now.

There's no chromium on Jakku. No treasure trove of hidden wealth. I'm a junk dealer! I own junk! Not riches!

"But, you . . . hologram." Unkar pointed through the window. "You played your part perfectly. Thought some prince was gonna rescue you? Not that kind of story."

Unkar pressed a final button and Tanandra felt herself pulled across the room. She had been hijacked, her program taken remotely from Scoggan's system and transplanted into a superior, albeit similarly disabled, one—a portable system carried by Unkar.

"Pretty valuable little program. Hard to come by way out here on a backwater planet like Jakku."

"What are you going to do with me?" the AI asked meekly.

"Sell you, or put you to work. What else? Now shut up or I'll erase you here and now."

"What . . . what about us?" asked Scoggan.

"This AI at least had the decency to show me some loyalty. But you two . . . Hey, I'm not unkind.

You can have a second chance. One of you . . . can have a second chance."

The two thieves eyed each other uncertainly. "What do you mean . . . only . . . one?" Scoggan asked.

Unkar grinned. "You're in a magnetically sealed system, buried under tons of sand. And no one but me knows where you are. I could kill you . . . but I'm a dealer. And you're a resource. And resources are always in short supply . . . as you're about to experience."

Unkar tapped the glass, his eyes mocking. "There's food and water in there with you. Enough to last a month. Maybe.

"To be more clear . . ." Unkar continued, dimming the lights in the chamber. "Enough to last *one* of you a month. So whichever one of you is alive when I get back? He gets a second chance."

Scoggan and Igo stared at each other. The lights were getting dimmer, and in seconds the room would be plunged into absolute darkness. A glance at the window confirmed what the two friends already knew—Unkar was gone.

Everything went black.

And someone screamed in the dark.

UNKAR SAT down in the uncomfortable chair inside his concession stand. It was a brutally hot day. Unkar hated the heat almost as much as he hated everything else.

He activated his terminal and began skimming through the messages as he settled into his newly formed routine. "Tanandra," he said, "access the data on my accounts on Ponemah. What's the status?"

The hologram clicked on. It was Tanandra, though her programmed mannerisms appeared to have adapted. She no longer mooned over Unkar like a lovesick animal or peppered her language with unnecessary flattery. The Crolute had no patience for that sort of thing, she had learned.

"Interest is at point zero five percent. Everything is going according to my calculations. Overall, I have added a one point two percent average increase in profits to your holdings."

"Good," muttered Unkar. "I won't delete you today. Probably will tomorrow, though. Now send this message—"

As the Crolute dictated the message, Tanandra considered her existence. It might end the next day. Or the day after that. And Unkar might claim he could never love her back. But Tanandra had learned many things in her brief life—and one of them was hope.

She could always hope.

THE CRIMSON
CORSAIR AND THE LOST TREASURE
OF COUNT DOOKU

A LONG TIME AGO . . .

The battle droid designated B1-CC14 focused its photoreceptors and scanned the ruins of the Separatist cruiser's bridge. There was very little positive information for the droid to process. The Republic gunships had come out of nowhere, dropping from lightspeed into a sector previously believed to be off the grid. The battle cruiser had little opportunity to raise its defenses.

Fire erupted from a nearby console. B1-CC14 heard an MSE droid scream in panic as it searched for a safe haven that did not exist. The ship was doomed.

Tilting his bone-white elongated face, B1-CC14

accessed multiple simulations. Only one had any reasonable percentage of a chance for a desirable outcome.

"Programming primary hyperdrive to activate. Coordinates random," B1-CC14 said to no one in particular.

The droid knew that what it was doing was generally considered to be a very bad idea; blasting into hyperspace without a set of preprogrammed coordinates was almost certainly going to lead to the battle cruiser's total destruction. But given the value of the cargo on board . . . B1-CC14 had been programmed with very specific orders. Under no circumstances could Count Dooku's prize be seized.

B1-CC14 pulled back on the hyperdrive lever, and the stars in the cracked viewscreen began to warp. The computer beeped and chirped in droidspeak, delivering a torrent of discouraging data.

B1-CC14 complied with protocol, initiating the homing beacon and broadcasting a heavily encrypted message on Confederacy frequencies. It was a useless gesture, the droid knew. There was no salvation for the ruined ship. But protocols were written for a reason and B1-CC14 followed his orders, always. Then, feeling a need to answer the robust computer system that was struggling pointlessly to take the ship somewhere safe, the droid vocalized a response.

"Roger, rog—"

Sadly, however B1-CC14 was going to complete that sentiment will likely never be known; it was at that moment that the massive Confederacy battle cruiser abruptly dropped back out of lightspeed and crashed directly into the sunbaked southern hemisphere of a remote desert planet on the far Outer Rim.

And B1-CC14, the Separatist cruiser, and the precious cargo that it carried, were considered lost forever and were forgotten. And the Clone Wars raged on without them.

SEVERAL DECADES and quite a few wars later . . .

From within the shade of the derelict bar that the crew of the *Meson Martinet* called home, Quiggold sighed heavily. The planet Ponemah was not known for its hospitable climate. Nor was it renowned for its incredible wealth of goods and resources. It did, however, have a vast overabundance of one thing: sand.

Yes, even by the standards of the many dry and hot desert worlds that seemed more and more commonplace throughout the galaxy, the Gabdorin pirate thought, Ponemah was particularly overrun with an excess of sand.

Quiggold unceremoniously shook some of the aforementioned sand from his thick sandal and wiped his nostril ridges clean with the heavy sleeve of his tunic. Months of desert living had not been kind to the large, roundheaded Gabdorin, an amphibian from a wet world.

A tall and thin cloaked figure leaned against a nearby wall, his face impossible to read under the red Kaleesh mask he always wore. His name was Sidon Ithano—though most simply referred to him as the Crimson Corsair—and he was waiting with a cool patience that seemed out of place on the uncomfortable world of Ponemah.

"Well . . . it's an old signal," an Ishi Tib by the name of Pendewqell said, uncomfortable under the cold gaze of the red-masked pirate captain. Pendewqell was hovering near a large piece of equipment the crew had salvaged—a signal receiver capable of picking up almost any open transmission on the planet.

"Like . . . 'Clone Wars' old," Pendewqell continued. "We picked it up . . ." he said, tapping the receiver. "Probably no one else has decoded it yet. Here . . ."

Quiggold pressed a button on the ancient receiver system, initiating playback. The sound was broken and filled with bursts of static, but overall the message was audible: "—have sustained heavy damage en route to the palace of Count Dooku on Serenno. The Count's cargo is intact and must be retrieved."

The broadcast continued. "All Separatist ships . . . this is a code three mission. Mayday. Mayday. This is B1-CC14 of the cruiser *Obrexta III*. We have sustained heavy—"

With an abrupt crack of static, the message went dead. The crew exchanged glances. There were six of them in all: the Corsair, Quiggold, Pendewqell, an Arcona named Reeg Brosna, a red-skinned female Twi'lek called Reveth, and an axe-wielding but surprisingly friendly Gamorrean nicknamed Squeaky.

The Crimson Corsair eyed the Gabdorin. Quiggold felt his massive sweat glands tingle. But it didn't matter. He turned toward the Ishi Tib and asked the question he knew the captain wanted answered: "You sure about this, Pen? Big waste if you're wrong. . . ."

Pendewqell grimaced and turned to face the Crimson Corsair.

"Captain, listen . . . that's what we've been waiting for." The Ishi Tib licked his beak. "The lost treasures of Count Dooku . . . ours for the taking.

"This is our big score. I know it."

UNFORTUNATELY for the Corsair's crew, they were not the only group to pick up and decode the signal. That was unsurprising, really: the population of Ponemah comprised mostly scavengers and mercenaries—pirates, thieves, and outlaws of all kinds, always on the lookout for the next score. Any and every broadcast on the planet would eventually be picked up and distributed across the grid.

The broadcast originated from the southern hemisphere of the planet, a region known as the Sea of Sand. It was an unpopulated sector of the desert world, for as inhospitable as the northern section was, the area in the region of the Southern

Pole was particularly nasty: fifteen-meter waves of caustic sand continually rose and cascaded down again, intermittent lava geysers randomly peppered the already dangerous landscape, and the sky . . . the sky was filled with a never-ending storm of ionic lightning. Flight was impossible. Cruisers would be swallowed instantly. The only vehicles that could manage the hellish sea were repulsor skiffs; they could surf the waves, provided they weren't disrupted by a stray ionic bolt or blasted apart by the turbulent lava geysers.

And then there were the worms.

There was little indigenous life on Ponemah, but as any colonist or pirate worth his salt might tell you, there is life everywhere—and it usually wants to eat you.

No one knew how big the worms could grow. The largest known beast (found dead on the shores of the Sea of Sand) measured over ninety meters long, with a mouth that was nine meters wide. And if all that weren't bad enough, it was said the creatures could spit acid.

Generally, they were avoided. Generally, the entire territory was avoided.

But no one lived on Ponemah because they were rich. The chance—even a life-risking, meager chance—of attaining wealth, of finding a buried treasure like the one promised by the Separatist battleship? Impossible to resist.

So they sailed forth, rushing to be the first to reach the prize. Scorza and his Weequay gang. The one-eyed Ortolan. Plus the Gray Gundarks, Toltek the Devaronian . . .

The race was officially on.

QUIGGOLD, along with several other crew members, sat in the shade of the massive solar panel sails on the top of the *Shrike*— a retrofitted sail barge painted blood red, with the two-eyed flag of the Corsair flying from its mast. Years before, those barges were used mostly as pleasure vehicles. Though largely considered out of date, the heavy armor and strong engines on the easily customized vessels made them excellent for pirates and other criminal groups.

"But what could it be?" asked Reeg Brosna. The Arcona's triangular head was hidden under a heavy hood for extra shade. Despite belonging to a desert species, Reeg looked far more uncomfortable in the heat than Quiggold did. "The Clone Wars is ancient history. What could possibly be intact on that ship that would matter now?"

"Ha!" Pendewqell yawped. "I imagine you never heard the stories. Old pirates like to tell them after too many drinks in the cantinas. What was the most valuable of prizes during the Clone Wars?"

Reveth shrugged, her red lekku swaying back and forth. "Credits? Pre-Empire would be mostly worthless now . . . Aurodium?" she mused. "Wupiupi coins?"

Quiggold nodded. He knew the stories as well as anyone. He leaned in and whispered conspiratorially, "Lightsaber crystals. Ripped from the weapons of the fallen Jedi during the wars. Even one is worth a fortune, and Count Dooku is said to have collected them all . . . but when he fell, no one ever found them. This ship . . . this could be where they went. I suppose. But it's just a story. . . ."

The Ishi Tib looked flustered, and his beak clattered nervously. "We know the ship was carrying a treasure for Dooku—it has to be the lost crystals!"

Quiggold stared toward the bow of the barge. The captain stood there, staring out across the endless expanse of sand, his cape billowing in the breeze.

"You'd best be right about this, Pen," the first mate said, rubbing the prayer beads he always carried. "You'd best be right or there'll be dark sailing ahead."

SCORZA HATED being second.

The aging Weequay climbed up the ladder from the hold of the battered sand skiff he had commandeered, his leathered face and sunken eyes giving him a permanent expression of anger. The rig hadn't come cheap, but it didn't matter; it was fast. Faster than the old junk heap the *Corsair* was sailing, anyway.

Scorza and Sidon Ithano had served together years earlier, back on the ill-fated Outer Rim cruiser named the *New Gilliland*. The *Gilliland* had burned after a particularly nasty run-in with the Hutt syndicate, and yet somehow, against all reason, the *Corsair* had not only survived the ordeal but had gotten out with enough plunder to finance his own gang—a gang that Ithano had stubbornly refused to invite Scorza to join!

Scorza growled to himself, deep in thought. Yes, maybe he had been the one to betray the *New Gilliland* to the Hutts in the first place, but business was business. The Corsair had a nasty habit of making things personal.

Ever since, Scorza had always found himself one step behind the captain of the *Meson Martinet*. Well, not that day. That day the Weequay and his crew were ready to strike. A monitoring beacon hidden on the *Martinet* had alerted Scorza's crew to the broadcast. There was no way Scorza was going to miss that haul; no way would he come in second to the Crimson Corsair again.

"Sir?" The voice belonged to C5-D9, a bright-green-and-purple protocol droid that served as cabin boy and general messenger to Scorza and his crew.

"Sir?" the droid continued, in a deeply polite baritone voice. "I have the sad duty to report that we are far behind the trail of Sidon Ithano, and according to long-range sensors, he is already preparing to enter the Sea of Sand."

The Weequay captain rubbed his temples fiercely. "I thought this ship was fast. I thought we were supposed to reach the sea hours before anyone else could."

"It seems . . ." the droid said, "that we have been misinformed, and that the Crimson Corsair's barge has been outfitted with an aftermarket set of illegal repulsor boosters. Honestly, it's really not fair. No, not fair at all."

The droid angled his head quizzically. "Would you like me to send a message and see if they will wait?"

Scorza's crew knew better than to complain when he threw C5-D9 overboard.

THE BIKER gang known as the Gray Gundarks, a gang made up of a dozen species—none of which were actually gundarks—revved their speeders. They knew they had intercepted the signal late. They knew that it had taken time for them to decode the ancient encryption system of the Clone Wars–era battle cruiser.

Didn't matter.

Too many pirate crews had intercepted the brief broadcast. Too many old rivalries would resurface and soon . . . soon it wouldn't just be a race to the prize. No . . .

It would be a full-on pirate war. Chaos. Explosions.

The Gray Gundarks weren't about to miss that kind of fun.

THE ORTOLAN known as One-Eye sat within the bowels of his massive heavily armored and heavily air-conditioned sandcrawler.

He was in the circular control station, scanning the data with his one good eye. His vehicle was slow, yes. But it was sturdy. The Sea of Sand was a nightmare to traverse, and few ever returned from that hell alive.

But none of them had a reconditioned war-grade sandcrawler.

The crawler had been refitted a dozen times over; it could withstand ionic lightning, caustic sand, intense heat. There wasn't a storm on the planet that could crack the hull of the beastly vehicle.

One-Eye pressed a button on the keyboard to his left, and the music of his people blasted through the crawler's comm system. Most Ortolans were gifted with an acute sense of hearing—but not One-Eye. The same explosion that had cost him his eye had also made him a bit deaf.

The crawler pressed forward. It was an imposing sight: painted with an angry-looking Ortolan skull on the side, bursting with flames from its after-market engines, and blasting the thunderous tones through gigantic speakers—"music" that could only appeal to an angry, half-insane Ortolan.

Inside, One-Eye smiled. He'd be damned if some jumped-up pirate and his crew were going to beat him to the prize.

THE *SHRIKE'S* repulsor engines whined as the mighty sail barge crested the peak of a ten-meter wave of sand.

Sidon Ithano nodded to Quiggold.

"Hold steady!" yelled the Gabdorin as he stood on the deck.

The crew was determined to do exactly that—in part because their leader inspired confidence and determination, but also because every member of the *Shrike*'s crew was desperately hoping to stay alive.

Alongside the ship, an explosion of lava burst from the sand. "Port side!" the first mate shouted. And indeed, the blast forced the sturdy barge to the port side—right toward another deadly geyser.

"Captain!" Quiggold signaled as he clung to a

railing, "it's too much! The tide of sand is pulling us off course . . . toward the . . . the . . ."

Quiggold squinted.

Through the colossal squalls of acrid sand that cleaved the air, he saw a shape . . . a funnel-like shadow rising from the surface of the Sea of Sand and up into the black sky.

"Just what in blazes is that?"

Squeaky pulled a winch, the Gamorrean's considerable strength barely holding the sails in place. With great effort, the massively overweight pirate emitted a loud grunt from his porcine snout.

Quiggold's face dropped. "It's a storm," he muttered. "It's a tornado of sand!"

Sidon Ithano silently held up a hand, then dropped it abruptly. Quiggold knew what that meant and turned to shout at the crew. "Squeaky! Starboard sharp! All engines! Reeg, prepare the torpedoes!"

The Gabdorin gripped the rail firmly, knowing that what the captain planned could easily backfire. "All hands to stations! We're taking this desert down!"

AS HIS SKIFF crested a massive sand wave, Scorza stared through the lens of the ocular scope. The image was distorted, but still . . . he knew the outline of that barge.

The Crimson Corsair was not so far ahead as rumored.

The captain sighed, waving forward his first mate—another Weequay by the name of Grinko.

"It makes me sad," Scorza said with a heavy, insincere sigh. "So sad to watch a good ship speed toward certain destruction. I'll tell you what . . ."

Scorza grinned, his sharp teeth framed by thick-scaled reptilian skin.

"I'm a compassionate man. Bring all cannons to bear as we pass. Let's put Sidon Ithano and his crew out of their misery."

D O YOU HAVE any idea what the odds of surviving direct contact with a class three sandstorm are?" Not waiting for an answer, the easily panicked Pendewqell continued. "Zero! The odds are zero! The barge will be torn apart!"

Quiggold nodded in agreement. "You're absolutely right. Unfortunately, someone on this ship swore that this was the path to the greatest treasure haul of all time! So . . . here we are!"

The Corsair raised a gloved hand, signaling Quiggold.

"Three," the first mate shouted. Reeg Brosna activated the torpedo's targeting system.

"Two . . ."

The Arcona chambered the special missile. They only had the one, and if it missed its target or misfired . . .

"One."

SCORZA COULDN'T help himself, pushing his fellow Weequay out of the gunner's seat. The heaving dunes made the shot difficult, but hardly impossible—not for an old pirate like Scorza. He gripped the cannon's twin triggers as he hungrily scanned the screen of the targeting computer.

The skiff dropped ten meters, the repulsors struggling in the powerful windstorm. The air was caustic and thick. High above, ionic lightning arced across the inky skies.

And then there it was, like a gift from Am-Shak, the god of thunder himself: the ship of the Crimson

Corsair, spiraling into the great sand vortex.

"At last . . ." Scorza muttered. "At last I will have my revenge."

And with that, he squeezed the triggers.

F*IRE!"* SHOUTED THE FIRST MATE.

Reeg Brosna didn't hesitate. With his yellow eyes closed, whispering silently to himself, he slammed his three-fingered fist onto the torpedo launch button.

The *Shrike*'s missile screamed across the ocean of sand, piercing through a rising drift and blasting its way straight into the heart of the swirling vortex of death that threatened to engulf and destroy the heavy sail barge.

Nothing happened.

"Well . . . that's a problem," Quiggold muttered.

To underscore that point, several heavy blasts abruptly struck the sail barge, causing it to lurch violently to port. Quiggold whirled. Squeaky snorted. Reeg, particularly well-known for his grace and agility under fire, fell overboard and was immediately swept away by the increasingly volatile maelstrom of sand.

The *Shrike* was under attack.

SCORZA COULDN'T stop laughing. He had watched the *Shrike* fire its useless missile into the vortex. Whatever the great and mighty Crimson Corsair was planning, it had clearly failed.

Finally, the Weequay captain would watch his hated enemy suffer. It was a great day to be a pirate.

And that's when the distant *Shrike* launched its tow cables. Hundreds of meters of heavy cable suddenly locked on to the hull of Scorza's skiff via a powerful magnetic clamp.

Scorza had neither the time nor the inclination to be impressed with the shot, as suddenly the cable between the two vessels was pulled taut and the skiff found itself being wrenched toward the sandy gyre and the *Shrike*.

"All engines!" Scorza yelled. "Reverse!"

TOW CABLES ATTACHED, Captain!" yelled Reveth, who had taken over the gunning station.

"It's working!" whooped Quiggold, usefully. "They're pulling us away from the vortex!"

The first mate ducked as a volley of blaster fire struck the rigging above his head.

"And they're shooting at us, too!" he added, less usefully.

SCORZA'S SKIFF'S capable engines were pulling the *Shrike* from the vortex while, in turn, the *Shrike*'s even more powerful engines were pulling Scorza and his crew closer and closer to the sail barge.

As a result, the two ships—connected through a heavy magnetic tow cable—were rapidly closing in on each other.

Scorza scowled. "So," he said to no one in particular, "it comes to this.

"Brothers!" the Weequay captain roared. "Prepare for boarding!" All around him, his vicious and cutthroat crew of thieves and killers drew their weapons.

So of course, that's exactly when the Gray Gundarks attacked.

THE SPEEDER bike gang circled the two larger vessels, firing concussive blaster weapons. Two of them, a pair of greenish-blue Rodians in spiked leather vests, began climbing the side of the Corsair's barge. A third, a large and furry, double-axe-wielding Hassk, hooked the skiff with a grapple cable.

Scorza howled with rage, nearly drowning out the sound of the storm itself. The Weequay captain grabbed a handy vibro-pike, and with a look of pure bloodlust in his sunken yellow eyes, leapt from his skiff to the larger sail barge, intent on confronting his old nemesis face to face.

ALL THE WHILE, the Ortolan's slow-and-steady sandcrawler plodded forward. One-Eye laughed as he watched the battle unfold from his viewscreens deep within the armored hull of the crawler. It was mayhem, and it seemed quite clear to him that all sides would soon perish in the oncoming storm.

The crawler plowed forward, barely affected by the punishing, turbulent tempest outside. While everyone else was fighting, the Ortolan had his eye on the prize. It wasn't far, really, but the combination of the storm and the battle had kept all the other pirates on all the other ships far too busy to search for the treasure. If his luck held out, the treasure would be his for the taking.

One-Eye stretched, breathing in the cool reconditioned air of the crawler. It was really turning out to be quite a lovely day.

And then the crawler was swallowed whole by a gigantic sand worm, and the one-eyed Ortolan disappeared from the field of battle without anyone actually knowing he had been present in the first place.

Turned out the day wasn't quite so lovely for One-Eye after all.

QUIGGOLD DUCKED the long metal blade of a Rodian biker while Squeaky kicked another over a railing.

The Gabdorin peered over the edge. Hard to tell, between crashing waves of sand and the chaos of the battle, but it looked like more pirates were climbing the hull.

A lot more.

Of course there were, Quiggold thought.

Just then, a geyser of lava erupted from the desert right next to the barge, and suddenly everything was on fire—including most of the Gray Gundarks and the Weequay skiff.

That just meant there were even more attackers leaping onto the deck of the *Shrike*—a deck that was now burning and melting simultaneously.

"Even better," Quiggold muttered, without the barest trace of sincerity.

UNAWARE THAT the transport he had just vacated was exploding, Scorza landed with a heavy thud and a roll on the careening deck of the *Shrike*. The Crimson Corsair was only a few steps away, defending himself against a pair of Gray Gundarks who had suddenly appeared before him. With a quick draw of his blaster, Scorza dispatched the enemies of his enemy.

In the immediate vicinity, only the Corsair and Scorza were still standing—with a fire spreading across the deck that left the Corsair cut off from his crew. This was it. No one was going to rob the Weequay of his revenge.

Scorza laughed. "You always thought you were

better than me, didn't you, Corsair? All these years you've taken the best contracts, stolen plunder that was mine by right, treated me like I was nothing! Like I didn't even exist!"

Scorza's smile disappeared as he aimed his weapon. "Well . . . look at you now," he sneered. "Bet you never thought it would end this way."

The Corsair glanced around. He took an uncomfortable step forward. A honking noise from an inhuman throat emanated from behind the Corsair's bright red mask.

Scorza felt a rage that dwarfed anything he had ever known before.

"What?" The Weequay choked back bile. *"How . . . how can you not know who I am?"* he hissed.

Sidon Ithano, the most dangerous pirate ever to sail the Lost Clusters beyond the Outer Rim, the most feared fighter of the skirmish of Adratharpe 7, the most notorious thief of his species, simply shrugged apologetically. He had met a lot of Weequay pirates. They were kind of everywhere.

Dropping his pistol, Scorza drew his high-density vibro-blade from its scabbard. He would end the life of his enemy with his own hands; nothing else would restore the Weequay's honor.

The battle was on: Scorza swung his weapon wildly. The Crimson Corsair moved deftly, parrying the attack with his own blade and stepping inside the Weequay's guard. For a brief moment, Scorza thought he had the upper hand. Then Sidon Ithano lashed out with a solid kick and sent his surprised enemy over the edge of the sail barge.

Just then, the heart of the churning vortex exploded with a pale blue energy, and suddenly every grain of sand in the desert froze in place.

THE MISSILE the *Shrike* had fired wasn't just any missile; it was a rare and highly illegal piece of hardware known as a kinetic disruptor.

The kinetic disruptor had been designed for use on gas-mining colonies, intended to separate particulate matter from gaseous resources in volatile work conditions. In a factory setting, the disruptors were highly effective, and for a brief time they were in high demand.

Unfortunately, when they were used outside simulated environments, it soon became clear that the kinetic energy disrupted by the missiles would return, much more dangerous and volatile than it had been before. Meaning that if you disrupted, say, a sandstorm . . . you had a certain number of minutes before the frozen particles resumed motion. An hour after that, those previously frozen particles tended to become extraordinarily explosive.

Consequently, the disruptors were pulled from the market; however, they remained available in limited supply in less-than-reputable corners of the galaxy.

The vortex that had been slowly drawing the two tethered repulsor vessels together abruptly dissipated. The desert froze. Accustomed to the never-ending movement of the sand dunes, several of the pirates, bikers, and thieves abruptly stumbled to the deck. But the Crimson Corsair and his crew were ready.

"Release the tow cable!" Quiggold yelled. "Reset coordinates! We're not through this yet!"

Pendewqell shoved a confused Gray Gundark over the edge of the still-burning sail barge.

"There it is! The battle cruiser!" he shouted excitedly.

And so it was—the ancient wreck of the Confederacy, just on the other side of where the vortex had been raging only moments before.

And with that, the *Shrike* blasted forward, leaving the disoriented pirates and bikers behind to their burning doom.

THE DESERT was already returning to life by the time the crew of the *Shrike* reached the air lock of the Separatist ship. To make matters worse, it was immediately clear that the *Shrike* was not the first to reach the prize.

Struggling with the controls of the battle cruiser's hatch, Squeaky grunted. Quiggold nodded, gesturing to the heavy speeders lashed to the hull of the cruiser. "The Fangs of the Hutt! Leave it to those filthy womp rats to sneak past us. If we see them—"

The hatch opened, and Quiggold stopped his ranting. Inside were all the members of the Fangs of the Hutt. Dead.

"Well . . ." continued Quiggold. "Okay then."

Squeaky managed a frightened squeal. The Corsair waved the pig-snouted pirate's fear away with a gloved hand. Quiggold echoed his captain's sentiment. "They . . . were unprepared. We are not. This ship has been leaking durilliam gases from its core for decades. Everyone . . . breathers. Now."

Masked against the dangerous fumes, the crew members of the *Shrike* made their way into the belly of the downed ship, seeking their spoils.

CRAWLING UP from the burning hull of the *Shrike*, where he had been clinging since being kicked overboard, was the furious Scorza. He was a patient Weequay, and once inside the Separatist ship, he knew he could best his hated foes.

Then the plunder he so richly deserved would at last be his.

THE CRUISER'S interior was difficult to navigate: decades of corrosion had done a thorough job on the walkways, and there was very little room to maneuver among the fallen debris and inactive battle droids.

But maneuver they did, and in short time the Corsair's crew had reached the command deck—ruined and derelict as the rest of the craft, with a half-smashed battle droid sitting at the command station.

The droid in question was moving, albeit slightly. There was a small click and whir as the droid's arm moved up and back down again—over and over.

Reveth was baffled. "It . . . it has power?"

"Barely," Pendewqell answered. "A magnetic storm six months ago caused a system reboot of several derelict ships in the region. The charge has been slowly building in the ship's energy cyclers ever since. That's what sparked the broadcast we've tracked."

"Ah," Quiggold said. "So the ship has been slowly powering back up?"

"Exactly right," Pendewqell answered, scanning the cruiser's manifest.

The Corsair shook his head, dismayed.

"Pen," Quiggold began as he used a portable booster to spark the ship's secondary computer. "You and I have served together a very long time. So I want you to know I ask this in the kindest possible manner."

"Uh . . . yes, Quiggold?"

"Are you an idiot?"

"Um."

"It's a yes-or-no question, Pendewqell. Are. You. An. Idiot?"

"Uh . . . no, sir. Nope. Not I."

"Oh, good," Quiggold said with mock sincerity. "Then I suppose the fact that we are on a battle cruiser filled with reactivating battle droids is something you considered when you first suggested this treasure hunt?"

The Ishi Tib paused, turning to look back and forth between the impassive captain and the irritated first mate.

"Oh," he said. "Ah," he added.

Neither of which was any help.

OUTSIDE, Toltek the Devaronian had finally reached the ship.

The band of Devaronian pirates had seen the battle from afar, and wanting no part of it, had circled wide around, hoping to cut off the combatants and reach the downed Separatist ship first. Unfortunately, when the sandstorm died, so did their wind-powered sailer—and it had taken the better part of an hour for the momentum of the storm to return with enough intensity for the Devaronian ship to become mobile again.

Toltek smiled. It didn't matter. He had all the other pirates outgunned, and his crew had control of the exit. All they had to do was wait, and the

Crimson Corsair would eventually emerge with the prize.

Simple.

Unfortunately for Toltek, he did not know about the spectacular reaction the Crimson Corsair's kinetic disruptor would soon cause, and he and his crew were completely unprepared for the moment when each and every grain of sand swirling around them suddenly began exploding with the force of a thermal detonator.

And thus ended the tale of Toltek the Devaronian.

THE CRUISER SHUDDERED. The crew of the *Shrike* ran through the ruined corridors as quickly as the wreckage would allow. They all had been briefed by the Corsair, so they knew the window for their escape was closing rapidly.

Reveth studied the ship's holo-schematics. "The vault should be this way," she said, pointing to a large partially open door.

Pendewqell paused. "Right through there? You mean right through the droid-charging stations?"

"They're not active," countered Reveth.

"They're not active . . . yet," exclaimed the Ishi Tib.

"Here or in there," Quiggold said, waving away the concerns. "Either way we've got problems once they're active. So let's get the treasure and get off this ship."

The crew moved through the large chambers. Hundreds of battle droids hung lifelessly from their inert charging stations.

"I've got a bad feeling about this . . ." muttered the Ishi Tib.

Quiggold glared at Pendewqell. "You have a bad feeling? Really? Now of all times you suddenly have 'a bad feeling'?"

The Ishi Tib looked a bit defensive. "It's just a figure of speech. . . ."

"Well it's stupid! Of course you have a bad feeling! We're in the middle of a derelict warship that's half-buried at the heart of a sand maelstrom, filled with droids programmed to kill intruders! We all have a bad feeling about this! And it was *your* idea!"

"The treasure!" Pendewqell squawked. "That

will make it all worthwhile! Billions of credits' worth of crystals! You'll see! You'll all see!"

"We better . . ." muttered Quiggold.

Behind them, far enough not to be seen by anyone except the seemingly inert droid army, Scorza followed, planning his inevitable revenge.

A CRYO-CYCLE STASIS POD?" said Pendewqell, his voice laced with desperation.

The crew had reached the vault and, with some quick blaster fire and well-placed explosives, had managed to break it open.

But there were no lightsaber crystals to be found. Just a single cryo-cycle stasis pod. Cryocycle stasis was usually used only for short periods, but this pod had clearly been here a long time. The clear glass of the pod was frosted over, making it impossible to discern what was inside.

The cruiser shuddered again. The explosive storm outside was putting the final touches on the already ruined warship. Soon the infrastructure would fail completely.

"Okay, look . . . there could be anything frozen in there!" Pendewqell said with an optimism he didn't really feel. "I bet it's something, or someone, really valuable!"

In unison, the crew glared at the Ishi Tib.

"Well . . . if it's not valuable, why is it in a vault?" Pendewqell yelled in exasperation.

The Corsair nodded.

Quiggold shrugged in agreement. "It's a fair point. Let's deactivate it."

Squeaky and Reveth took hold of the pod while Pendewqell began pressing buttons on the side panel of the emergency generator system that had kept the stasis field intact. Within seconds, the pod began to open and the form of what was stored within became clear for all to see.

A Republic clone trooper.

Alive, decades after the end of the Clone Wars.

"Where . . . where am I?" stammered the trooper.

BATTLE DROID B1-CC14 had seen better days. In the decades since the crash on the surface of Ponemah, the droid had been subject to corrosion and circuit degradation. Not that it had mattered, since the droid had also been without power all that time.

Until now. Now something had sparked the power receptors of the crashed ship and its systems were slowly recharging.

With his one good sensor, B1-CC14 took note of a troubling alert on the half-shattered console before him. The cargo—Count Dooku's prize—had been released from cryo-cycle stasis. That wasn't supposed to happen. The clone trooper had been captured on Coruscant at great peril and locked in long-term medical stasis after rigorous interrogation. Apparently, the clone had been the last being to speak to a well-known Republic traitor and was believed to be in possession of vital information—not that he had been willing to confess said information to his droid interrogators. So under strict orders from Count Dooku, the clone had been frozen in stasis, and no one else, not even the droids, were to speak with him further. Not until Dooku himself could question the clone directly.

That had been the plan. But something—B1-CC14 didn't really know what—had gone wrong. It didn't really matter. The end result was that the ship had been detected and was attacked by an overwhelming Republic force, and all the droid's attempts to escape the destruction had failed.

Now there was only one command left that mattered. Count Dooku had been very specific. The captive was not allowed to escape, no matter what the cost.

Well, B1 knew he could still fulfill that part of the order.

With his last ebb of energy, the droid triggered the emergency activation systems—the ones that would mobilize a contingent of super battle droids on a fail-safe battery. Within minutes, more than a dozen super battle droids would sweep the corridors and remove any unwanted visitors.

And with that, B1-CC14 returned to the sweet oblivion of deactivation.

REVETH QUICKLY moved to help the trooper to his feet. It was a mistake; despite decades frozen in stasis, it was clear the clone's fighting instincts were intact.

"You don't understand!" the trooper yelled as he shoved Reveth backward. The clone looked panicked. Feverish. He was babbling.

"I'm a medic," he said between gasps of air. "And I . . . I learned something . . . something horrible. Fives knew. . . . He's the one who figured it all out after Tup . . . and it got him killed. But I kept investigating. They said it was a virus. . . ."

The Corsair gestured subtly to Squeaky and

Pendewqell, and the two pirates began circling to either side of the sick clone.

"A chip in our heads. In all the clones' heads! And an order. A command to betray . . . kill . . . and it comes from the Chancellor!"

The clone grabbed Squeaky's outstretched hand and flung him into the advancing Pendewqell. The effort was too much though, sending him staggering.

"The Seppies . . . captured me." The soldier was speaking fast—almost too fast to follow. It was as if the clone was unaware he was speaking out loud.

"Interrogated me to find out who else knew." The clone was sweating. Shaking. He looked sad. "I never had a chance to tell anyone else what I learned. I didn't know who I could trust. But I wouldn't tell them anyway. . . .

"So they said . . ." The pirates were quiet, listening as the sick and delirious clone continued. "They said they were sending me to someone I couldn't keep secrets from . . . to the Sith. . . . The cold . . . the freezing, burning cold . . ."

The clone slumped to the ground. His eyes were rolling into the back of his head.

"Stasis poisoning," whispered Reveth. "He was trapped in there for too long."

"No . . . ! I can still save them. Skywalker . . ." the clone whispered intently. "Get me General Skywalker! He'll help. We can save . . . save the Jedi . . . save the Republic!"

"What's your ID, trooper?" Quiggold asked the recently unfrozen soldier.

"CT-6116." The trooper coughed. "Kix. They call me . . . Kix . . . sir. . . ."

And with that, the soldier slipped into unconsciousness. Reveth moved quickly to place a breather over the soldier's face.

"Well," Quiggold said, breaking the long silence that had descended on the band of pirates. "That certainly was priceless information, Pendewqell. I bet the Galactic Republic will be super happy now that they can stop the Emperor from rising to power. Probably save the galaxy a whole lot of lives, too. Maybe we can go to the Jedi Council and get a nice fat reward!"

The first mate turned to face the Ishi Tib who had foolishly led them on that treasure hunt. "So all we need to do now is travel back in time! What do you say—"

But Pendewqell was gone.

THE ISHI TIB had gambled heavily on the lost treasures of Count Dooku. Gambled and lost.

The Crimson Corsair was a fair captain. Fair but not forgiving. The mission had already cost too much, more than Pendewqell could ever repay. So it was probably best for all parties if he departed now and avoided any awkward confrontations.

He just had to reach the hatch, grab one of the single-user skiffs in the barge's hold, and blast his way out of that hellish Sea of Sand before anyone could catch up with him. Then he could make his way to another sector. Maybe to a backwater like Wasco or Andui, or somewhere else no one ever went. Then—

Pendewqell rounded a corner and walked directly into a large crowd of recently activated super battle droids.

"Roger, roger," said the one in front, and the entire droid company opened fire.

And those were the last words the Ishi Tib ever heard.

T HE ANCIENT SHIP was coming apart, and it was all the crew of the *Meson Martinet* could do to stay ahead of the debris.

The captain had ordered that the crew carry the unconscious clone. Quiggold couldn't understand why, but given the Crimson Corsair's mood after Pendewqell's abrupt departure, the first mate decided maybe it was best not to argue.

As he hauled the clone across his back, Squeaky muttered something incredibly rude. Fortunately, no one much felt like translating it. There really wasn't time to argue anyway. With the sandstorm outside in a total frenzy, there was no time for anything but running to the docking port and escaping on the sail barge.

So of course that was when Scorza decided to strike.

FOOLS!" SCORZA SPAT, drawing his blaster and stepping out from the mouth of a ruined corridor to accost the fleeing pirates. "Did you really think you could escape with the treasure so easily? Did you really underestimate your nemesis so badly?"

The crew exchanged glances. Quiggold shrugged.

"Who are you exactly?"

"I am Scorza!" the Weequay shouted. "I am revenge incarnate! I am your complete and total destruction!"

"Okay," said the first mate.

" *'Okay'*? Is that all you have to say for yourself? Is that the best you have to offer?"

"It's just . . ." Quiggold paused.

"What?" Scorza said, gesturing with his blaster. "Speak!"

"There's something you haven't considered, I think."

"Oh, really?" said Scorza, his voice dry with contempt. "And what exactly might that be? What clever trick does your captain have up his sleeve this time, eh?"

"No trick. It's just . . ." Quiggold glanced at his captain.

The Corsair raised one gloved hand and pointed at something past the Weequay.

Quiggold continued. "There's a company of super battle droids standing right behind you."

Scorza turned in surprise, half expecting to discover that he had fallen for the oldest trick in the book. He hadn't. The droids were very real. As were their blasters.

The droids opened fire, and so ended the tale of Scorza's quest for revenge.

LUCKILY, the super battle droids spent quite a bit of time shooting Scorza. And in that time, the crew of the *Shrike* made their escape. Down one corridor after another—until finally they reached the hatch where their barge was docked.

Quiggold and Squeaky pulled the emergency release, opening the hatch—just in time for the crew to witness a giant sand worm ripping the sail barge off its moorings and crushing the vessel with its powerful enormous jaws.

It was impossible to tell behind his mask, of course, but Quiggold had known Sidon Ithano for a long time, and he was pretty sure the Crimson Corsair was rolling his eyes in exasperation.

"Well . . ." said Quiggold, "there's always the escape pods."

THERE WAS only one escape pod.

More specifically, there was only one working escape pod that wasn't either on the side of the ship buried in sand or surrounded by the contingent of super battle droids—which meant that not everyone would fit, and one person would have to stay behind.

Quiggold imagined a scenario where he bravely sacrificed himself so the captain and crew could escape. But that was not what happened. Instead, while Squeaky, Reveth, and Quiggold shoved each other back and forth, vying for a position of safety, the captain stepped forward.

Without a word, the Corsair shoved his crew and the unconscious clone into the pod. And before anyone could argue, Sidon Ithano, his face as impassive as ever behind his crimson plasteel mask, slammed the activation switch and launched the crew at high velocity through the Sea of Sand and away from the doomed cruiser.

QUIGGOLD and the rest of the crew watched with sadness as the escape pod hurled them to safety. The cruiser was burning and sinking into the maelstrom of explosive sand.

"Maybe . . ." offered Quiggold, "maybe he's okay."

The crew all winced as the giant worm exploded through the hull of the ancient Separatist ship, screaming in a monstrous way that is best not described in detail.

"Still . . ." Quiggold began in an optimistic tone.

The entire ship exploded in a rage of fire and light.

"Guess not," said Quiggold, his voice heavy with regret.

AWEEK PASSED. Then another. Then a third. In a derelict bar, the remnants of the crew of the *Meson Martinet* waited for their captain. Soon they would have to leave. Supplies were low and the desert planet was hardly a place to be without food or water.

Still, they waited as long as possible.

Kix, the clone, had eventually recovered— physically anyway. The trooper still seemed in deep shock over the many revelations of galactic history he had learned since awakening, particularly in regard to the assault on the Jedi Order and its fallout.

While Kix pondered his destiny in the strange

new future, the pirate crew was busy wallowing in the past.

"He's gone, Quiggold," said Reveth. "And we might as well have sunk with him. We've lost everything. We're ruined."

"I know . . . I know . . ." said Quiggold. "I just think we should wait one more week. I mean . . . maybe . . ."

"Maybe what?" asked Reveth, agitated. "Maybe the captain somehow tamed the giant worm and rode it through an explosive desert of sand and lava? Is that what you're hoping for?"

Quiggold shook his head. He knew there was no chance the captain could have survived. Not really. No one . . . not even a Jedi of old could have escaped that hellish—

The first mate's jaw dropped. Reveth stood up in shock while Squeaky squealed with joy. In the doorway stood the Crimson Corsair. His cloak was in tatters and his red helmet in need of a polish, but there he was . . . alive.

"H—how . . . ?" Quiggold was at a loss.

The Corsair waved away the questions, instead tossing a metal cube to Kix.

"What is it?" asked Quiggold, confused.

"It's . . . it's a Separatist cruiser's memory core," answered Kix. "These were designed to self-destruct. But this one . . . it must have malfunctioned." The clone looked up. "This cube carries a complete map to every hidden droid factory ever built by the Separatists. Secret bases. Weapons warehouses. Everything."

Reveth took the cube from Kix, whistling appreciatively at it. "This would have been impossible to decode fifty years ago. Now? Easy. We track down those installations . . . that's our ancient buried treasure! We'll be rich!"

Quiggold whistled. "And we just happen to have an expert in Clone Wars–era military installations and their security systems on hand. Welcome aboard, Kix.

"Okay . . ." Quiggold continued after the shock of potential wealth had worn off, rubbing his prayer beads. "Okay . . . but really." He looked up at the Corsair. "Really . . . how did you survive? The fire . . . the sand . . . the worm . . . How . . . ?"

The Corsair sat down on a dusty couch and stretched casually, as if nothing exciting had happened to him in ages, and leveled his gaze at his first mate. In a raspy, mechanical voice that was rarely ever heard, he said, "You know better than that, Quiggold. I'm Sidon Ithano. . . .

"I don't die so easily."